BRIDGES AND BODIES

T.A. HUGGINS

EN TIME MYSTERY

RIDGES
ODIES

bitat
Humanity
insula and
ater Williamsburg

manity Peninsula
g since 2006.

g-back

ANCOUVER

BRIDGES AND BODIES : A Ben Time Mystery

Published in New York, New York, by Morgan James Publishing. Morgan James is a trademark of Morgan James, LLC. www.MorganJamesPublishing.com

ISBN 9781642793741 paperback
ISBN 9781642793758 eBook
Library of Congress Control Number: 2018914256

Cover Design by:
Megan Dillon
megan@creativeninjadesigns.com

Interior Design by:
Chris Treccani
www.3dogcreative.net

Morgan James is a proud partner of Habitat for H
and Greater Williamsburg. Partners in buildi

Get involved today! Visit
MorganJamesPublishing.com/givi

TABLE OF CONTENTS

PREFACE

I have listened to many narratives concerning incidents that have occurred on many a train trip. I am married to a retired railroad engineer. I have changed to some degree the facts so as not to embarrass, incriminate, or undermine those involved (mainly my husband). I have tried to be true to the workaday life involved in modern railroad employment. In this book, the towns of Avon and Danville and their railroad bridges are real; however, the incidents surrounding the towns and bridges are not. These incidents and characters are fictional products of my imagination. Any resemblances to actual events, organizations, or persons, living or dead, are coincidental.

The haunted bridge in Avon, Indiana has been memorialized in numerous paintings and is pictured on the town seal of Avon. If you would like more information about the bridges you can go to the following websites: *www.visithendrickscounty.com search Haunted Bridge of Avon,* and *https:/.en.m.wikipedia.org>wiki> Ghost Legends of Indiana.*

Finally, the facts concerning mandatory drug testing on the railroad were gathered from *www.en.m.wikipedia.or>wiki>1987 Maryland train collision.*

ACKNOWLEDGMENTS

I would like to acknowledge my husband, who dutifully reads and rereads the entire manuscript for railroad technicalities. He put in his nearly forty years of railroad service only to retire and become my faithful proofreader. Thank you, dear, for your love, expertise, and help. I would also like to thank my editor, Lisa Lickel, for her work, suggestions, and kind words of encouragement. In addition, I would like to give a big thanks to John Minton for his telling of the corn syrup incident. I can only hope that my retelling has done it justice. Morgan James Publishing; my Acquisitions Editor, Terry Whalin; Angie Kiesling, the Fiction Editor; and Gayle West, Author Relations Manager; were also invaluable with their suggestions and encouragement as we moved from manuscript to the final product. Finally, I want to always include a hallelujah for my Savior and Lord, who guides and directs my path.

CHAPTER 1

SAINT LOUIS, MARCH 18, 0800 EST

He entered the hotel dining room like a bull, roaring out my name. "Ben, Ben, I just heard we may be here for a while or the opposite, deadheaded, taking a van ride, home early."

I swiveled in my seat to see the source of all the commotion. It was none other than Indiana, fellow engineer, once pain in my side, now faithful yappy puppy friend.

"Ben, did you hear about the derailment?"

"I haven't heard a thing. Just got seated and started on my first cup of coffee. Take a load off and join me for breakfast Indiana, and you can spill the beans."

"I thought you would be skipping breakfast. I heard your wife has you on another diet."

"That rumor has to be about some other guy. I am at my peak," I said as I patted my rounded stomach.

Indiana ignored me and began his explanation of the derailment. "The eastbound mail train E206 on track number two just hit a knuckle and bam, first four cars and the locomotive went on the ground. That coupler had to have been bad, you know? Otherwise the connection, the knuckle, wouldn't have busted. Several more cars were spread out on both track number two eastbound and track number one westbound and several more were over in the swamp. The environmental guys will be all over the railroad with the diesel fuel having spilled out of the locomotive into the swamp water. It's a mess. All rail traffic has been stopped for at least twenty-four hours, I'd say. Earlier last night the westbound Bone Crusher W676 train with Ty and the Mad Russian were on track number one headed to St Louis and they had a problem when their train went into emergency application while leaving Terra Haute. MR, the Mad Russian, walked the track looking for the knuckle that had snapped in two."

"That has happened to me as well. The knuckles are aging and can't take the stress."

Indiana continued. "The strange thing is that he didn't find it. MR said there was a lot of slack action in that train, too many long draw bars with heavy boxcars. The weight caused too much strain on the knuckle and it broke. After the Russian walked the train he reported to the dispatcher that he could not find the missing piece and he replaced the missing knuckle with an extra one mounted on the lead locomotive. The two of them made it to St. Louis before dying or running out of time set by the Federal government in the yard. I don't think a track inspector was called out to search for the missing knuckle."

"Of course not."

"The train dispatcher wanted to get the mail train through Terra Haute since it was already late and held up by the Bone Crusher's problems. He didn't want to wait on the track inspector so he just kept the mail train moving."

"That's par for the course of management."

"After the derailment, part of a knuckle was found lodged in the old bakery switch on the eastbound track. The knuckle caused the derailment of the E206 mail train. Rumor has it that the railroad pulled the train dispatcher out of service for not getting the track inspected before letting E206 come through town. They're waiting for Ty and the MR to be rested and then will consider pulling them out of service. They have the crew of the E206 in the yard office grilling them now."

"Was anyone hurt?" I asked.

"I was told that the crew was okay. You know how they love to blame us trainmen, Ben."

"All too well," I said as I slurped up another mouthful of coffee. "And you're probably right that they'll either leave us here at the hotel longer or deadhead us home. I guess it'll depend on where more trains get stacked up, here, in Saint Louis, or back in Indianapolis."

"Since I'm betting I'll have some time here at this end, I'm going to visit the boat. See ya later," Indiana shouted as he stood, pushed in his chair, and marched out.

The dining room got very quiet once again.

As I sipped at the coffee I thought about our new-found friendship, Indiana and me. I've been working on the railroad for thirty-some years. He worked there longer. Most of my service has been in the transportation department working with the trains, first as a brakeman, then conductor, then engineer. I thought that most of Indiana's service was in transportation as well, but that's where any similarities between the two of us ended. Just last year Indiana was my arch nemesis, targeting my faith whenever there was a group of trainmen and he could be the center of attention. He had multiple wives and multiple child support payments, drank, gambled, and was accused of murdering a train master less than a year ago.

I didn't believe he was the murderer, visited him in jail, and prayed with the man. He's been a loyal friend ever since then—since we discovered who really committed the murder. Indiana hadn't completely changed his ways, as the boat he was headed to was the casino boat. However, he hadn't been complaining as much, hadn't even begun to deride me for my faith as of late, and seemed to be generally easier for every one of the guys to get along with.

Interrupting my thoughts, the waitress returned with my breakfast, two eggs over easy, bacon cooked crisp, and jelly toast. I stopped thinking about Indiana and put my thoughts and actions into the meal placed before me.

I ate quickly since I had no company to sidetrack me. I sat and finished my third cup of coffee then decided it would be a good idea to stop in the fitness room and get a mile in on the treadmill.

The fitness room television was blaring out the news, another robbery at a nearby gas station, two teenagers with guns. At least this time, no one was killed. There was one other man, a fellow exerciser with head phones on, riding the stationary bike. I stepped up on the treadmill, placed the safety clip on my shirt, and began a slow-paced walk. The fitness room door opened and in moved my friend and favorite conductor, Lurch, with one long stride.

"Hi, Big Ben," he said with a broad smile on his six-foot, seven-inch frame.

"Hi, Lurch," I replied between breaths as my speed picked up a notch. "Did you see Indiana yet this morning?"

Lurch nodded in the affirmative. "I did. He told me all about the derailment and he hurried to his taxi. He's off to the boat, I assume. I hope he makes it back in time in case we're the crew deadheaded home early."

"Me too. He doesn't need to get in more trouble. I'm hoping it will be us, though, that'll be deadheaded home early. I could use some home time." I puffed out the words as I walked.

"Did you eat?"

"Yep, I'm trying to get rid of breakfast as we speak."

"Okay, I'll leave you to reduce and go get my breakfast. Talk later," Lurch said as he backed out of the fitness room and shut the door.

I was almost at one quarter mile when Lurch exited. Exercise always passed by quickly if there was someone to talk to. Thinking I might just get two miles in since the first quarter mile passed by so rapidly, I quickened my pace yet again. I could now hear the fellow exerciser on the bicycle breathing heavily. His legs were pumping like an engine moving through a clear signal. He was definitely in better shape than I was. I continued with the accelerated pace, huffing and staring at the television. Peer pressure had affected my usual good sense of walking at a leisurely stroll. As I finished up my two miles, my phone went off with the "Don't Worry Be Happy" ring tone I used to identify incoming work calls. I huffed out, "Ben Time."

A human voice responded with, "Mr. Time, you are being deadheaded back to Indianapolis at 1100 EST." Our calls are always announced in Eastern Standard Time to avoid confusion since our railroad crosses two time zones.

"Thanks, looking forward to the ride home." I placed my phone back in my pocket with a cough and left the fitness room to get ready for the van ride home. Once up in my room, I brushed my teeth and placed my few toiletries in my bag I was thinking of calling my wife to warn her that I would be home about 1600 hours. If I didn't get the deadhead home I wouldn't get home until the following day sometime. Deb usually expected that I would be gone for three days when called out on a trip. Trainmen on this run, Indianapolis to Saint Louis, didn't have scheduled trains. We were on call night and day, seven days a week, and holidays. More trains ran at night than in the day but with twelve hours on duty, our scheduled work time limit set by the federal government, our trips often cross day to night and vice versa. The lack of schedule was hard on the body. My doctor and my wife advised me to retire as soon as possible. I planned on taking their advice.

I had another hour before I needed to report to the van for the trip home so I turned on the TV and found an old rerun of *Texas Rangers* to occupy my time. I was thinking that maybe when I retire I would take a trip out west, when I was startled by a knock on the door. I got up guessing it would be Lurch only to find Rocko, my conductor this trip, standing there with a cup of coffee in his hand.

"What's up, Rocko?" I asked as he sipped his coffee.

He swallowed hard, looked at his watch, and asked if I knew about the derailment and if I received the call to deadhead home.

I responded in the affirmative, took note of his very expensive watch, and asked him into the room. He shook his head in the negative and strode down the corridor.

I shut my door and started to guess at the character of my new conductor, Rocko. Rocko was new to our pool, the term that describes a group of trainmen assigned to the same run. He came up to Indianapolis two months ago. He had enough seniority to bump on this pool. That meant that one conductor with less seniority got bumped from the pool. The process upset the applecart and made everyone suspicious of the new guy. It was just the union rules of the game and I tried and give the new guy a break.

Rocko was not very responsive to kindness. I tried with some small talk on the trip from Indy to here but his responses were short, to the point, or none at all. I had guessed that it was due to being treated with some hostility by some of the other engineers and conductors. He was suspicious of all of us, too. Some of the old guys on the pool would exaggerate any mistakes made by the new guy or just plain lie and belittle the new guy's abilities. It took a while to fit in on a pool. Each pool was kind of like a gang. You had to pass through an initiation to be accepted. Sometimes it meant that the new guy would be physically threatened by some of the mouthier guys on the pool. But, it usually resulted in much talk and no action. I surmised that Rocko stopped by to either warn me about the work call or make sure I would be in the van on time.

I looked at the clock on the bedside table and realized I still hadn't called my wife to give my usual warning call. So, I called home. I got Deb's answering message and left her a message indicating my early arrival. I grabbed my grip and headed to the hotel foyer. I told the front desk girl, Amy, to have a good day and exited the sliding glass doors and headed to the minivan, my ride home.

CHAPTER 2

SAINT LOUIS, MARCH 18, 1100 EST

saw that Rocko was already in the van and had taken the front seat. I would really rather have the front seat for the four-hour plus trip home but, as they say, "losers weepers." Our drivers received new minivans, we railroad crewmen called limos, this past year but the middle two seats were very uncomfortable for an old sod like myself. I threw my grip into the back of the van and folded myself into travel position.

"Hi Betty," I said while adjusting my seat.

"Hey, Big Ben," she responded in her deep, somewhat hoarse voice. Betty's voice betrayed her biggest vice, she was a smoker of some sixty-some years. I knew Betty was in her seventies and had shuttled railroaders around for at least twenty years. She could handle the hottest tempered of trainmen. In addition, she drove better than most of the rail limo drivers. I appreciated her. "How is the limo business?" I asked.

"Long hours, little rest. Kind of like the rail business. But you guys get much better pay."

"We shuffle thousands of pounds of freight, Betty, not two little guys like Rocko and myself." I laughed at my own joke. Betty chuckled and put the minivan in gear for our trip home. I noticed that Rocko didn't chuckle, tee hee, or say a word.

It was March and Betty commented on the strange weather. It was twenty-nine degrees yesterday morning and today it was sixty degrees. The sun was out. This was often a tease that spring was just around the corner. The grass was still straw colored, not bright green, full of water and life yet. We had had two tornado watches already this spring. Betty and I both agreed that the weather had been much more violent the past couple of years. In the violent storms, I feel the safest in the locomotive. The funneling winds have moved the freight cars but rarely an engine.

Betty and I discussed the weather for some time. Rocko never added a word to the conversation. I didn't want to leave him out so I addressed him directly. "Rocko, have you ever been in a tornado?"

He responded with, "No," and said nothing more.

I saw Betty turn her head slightly and give Rocko a look of reproach as she reached for a hard candy. She couldn't smoke while transporting us so hard candy filled the void.

I took a long look at the back of Rocko's head. He had nearly black hair spotted with a few grays. It reminded me of the time I was cleaning paper strings off our driveway after my daughter's birthday party. I didn't get all the kinky white paper threads with the broom. The few remaining stood out on the black surface. My wife came out of the house and said, "Missed a few." My mind often wandered on road trips where I wasn't in control of the vehicle.

I drew my attention back to my new conductor. I estimated his age to be in his fourth decade. He was about my height, five feet, eight inches tall, average build, slighter than my paunchy build. His face had some scars from past acne that had not been treated. I continued thinking that the newer medications were a blessing for those who suffered from acne. They no longer have to face the daily ridicule and scarring that lasted a lifetime. I wondered if Rocko had faced ridicule as a teen.

I had asked him on our trip over to Saint Louis how he came to bump on this pool. He said he could make more money here and that business was waning on the Evansville pool.

Business was up and down on most pools so I guessed that there was more to the decision to move than just that. The expense of moving to a new area, the uncertainty of business on any pool, and the experience of rough treatment from trainmen keeps bumping down to a minimum.

My mind was wandering because Betty announced that she was ready to pull off the road and fill up the vehicle, our halfway point. This was also code for "I need a smoke." I was ready for a stretch. I hobbled out of the minivan and into the convenience store. My stomach was making some disturbing sounds so I looked for something to quiet it. After several rounds of searching the store for my desired lunch I decided on a ham salad sandwich and a diet cola. I really wanted chips but I held back thinking I might brag a bit to my wife about my newfound self-discipline in food choices. I crawled into the backseat and while waiting for the return of my fellow passengers I unwrapped my lunch.

Betty returned first, refreshed by a nicotine fix, also carrying a sandwich and cola. We both saw Rocko approaching the van; however, he carried no nourishment with him. Once Rocko was seated and belted in Betty put her foot to the gas pedal and we returned to the interstate. The traffic consisted, for the most part, of tractor trailers carrying their miscellaneous freight along the I-70 corridor. The summer construction season had not begun yet so we wouldn't be delayed by the single lanes consisting of long lines of marching turtles and trailers. Betty and I were happily silent as we partook of our cuisine while cruising along. Rocko was just silent through the entire state of Illinois.

All was quiet for some time. As we traveled through Indiana, Betty asked, "What do you know about the haunted railroad bridge near the yard, Ben?"

"I heard quite a few stories about the bridge across County Road 625 and White Lick Creek when I first moved to Indianapolis. The ghost stories varied quite a bit from haunted by an Irish construction worker to haunted by a distraught mother. I googled it one night and found the date the bridge was constructed was not known for certain but seemed to be from the late 1850s to early 1900s. One website dated it as built in 1906. The bridge, itself, is impressive. It's three hundred feet long and seventy feet high. It is a triple arch bridge. It's double tracked with a walk along its side. The bridge crosses County Road 625 and the White Lick Creek. In fact, the structure is so impressive the town uses the bridge on its town seal."

Betty interrupted. "Is it haunted? You guys cross it all the time."

"I have yet to see a ghost or hear a ghost. But they say if you cross it at night you may hear moanings by one to three ghosts. And if you cross it in the summer when it's a hot day you may see ghost tears on the rails.

"The sources of the moanings are accounted for by three stories online. So, you take your pick of the one you prefer. One story goes like this. A man by the name of Henry Johnson was an alcoholic construction worker and while working on the bridge in the 1800s he fell into the wet cement and dried there overnight. Another story goes that an Irish construction worker fell inside a support and since he was dead the railroad left him there and poured cement right over him. The man's arm hung out so they cut it off."

Betty replied, "Sounds like the railroad," and coughed.

I agreed and continued on with the third story. "A mother was walking across the bridge with a sick baby in her arms attempting to get to a doctor. She got her foot caught between the ties and a locomotive advanced upon her. She didn't have enough time to get across so she jumped the seventy feet with her baby in her arms. This was long before there was a walkway built along the tracks. She survived but the baby did not. Several weeks later she died of a broken heart.

"Those are the three stories accounting for the moanings and tears. There are some slight variations in the stories when you look them up on the internet and several additional stories. They are all quite sad. I have never heard any moaning above the noise of the locomotive engines. It would have to be a very loud ghost indeed for trainmen to hear it!"

Betty laughed, "Everyone knows trainmen are hard of hearing. Those are sad stories. I wonder if there is any truth to them."

"I have no idea, Betty, no idea," I replied.

Once again, I noticed that Rocko was alive, not sleeping, by the movement of his head, but he didn't take part in the conversation. Betty and I quieted for the rest of the trip. The last half hour went by quickly as we were returned to the Indianapolis yard. I usually walk in with the conductor while he puts in our time slips. But when Rocko got out of the van and took several steps he was stopped by Sudsy, the conductor who was bumped off our board when Rocko bumped on. I saw that the exchange was not going to be pleasant so I just walked over to my truck, threw my grip in, and left for home.

Sudsy, like most trainmen, goes by his nickname. He received this particular name because he was caught midway through a shower when the hotel lost its water supply several years back. He came down to the foyer ranting and raving with his hair still in suds. On the railroad, trainmen rarely use their true names, but rather, the name given or earned, or not, by other trainmen. I was thinking that I'd have to ask Rocko why he carried his moniker since I believed his real name was James Rice.

Sudsy was angry when he had approached Rocko, there was no doubt of that fact. I read his body language. His arms were flying, his face in a scowl, and his voice loud. I could hear the loud volume of his tenor voice over the high-pitched retarders in the yard. I couldn't make out his words. He should have let go of his rage by now over being bumped from the Saint Louis pool. It was a union rule. It protected positions based on seniority. He'd been working long enough to know the rules and suffer the consequences.

I looked at my watch and saw it was 1630 hours. We made good time from Saint Louis. I could be home in ten minutes ready to kick off my shoes.

I entered my house yelling, "Mertle, I'm home." I call her Mertle just so she knows it's me. Her real name is Deb, Dr. Deb is how she is known to her students. I married up. She has put up with me for thirty-some years now and raised our two daughters, often alone, due to my time away from home working the rails.

She hollered back, "I'm in the spare bedroom."

I had taken off my work boots out in the garage so as not to track creosote from the railyard into the house. Deb had complained that I left a trail of debris on every flat surface in the house as I made my way toward our bedroom. I told her that's how I find my way back out. She doesn't always enjoy my fine sense of humor.

I found her in the spare bedroom hanging curtains.

"Hi, Ben, how was your return trip?" she asked as she straightened the last panel.

"It was uneventful and we made good time in the minivan," I replied.

"I washed these curtains today and I'm getting them hung back up so they'll wrinkle less. Do you want to go out for dinner?"

"I sure do. Give me a minute to change my clothes and I'll be ready to go out with my favorite girl," I said, as I turned to leave the spare room and headed toward our bedroom.

We decided to go to the diner in the same small town in which our church is located. The diner is known for its great catfish. We waited about ten minutes for our table, sat, ate and talked about some new developments in our youngest daughter Liz's job situation. She was expecting to change jobs within the same hospital. We went straight home after dinner so I could get some rest. Since I was deadheaded home I would be out soon to take a train west. The trains would be backed up and the board, or list of engineers and conductors assigned to the same pool, would be moving through names quickly.

When we arrived at home I got comfortable in my recliner and began my usual channel surfing. Deb went to the spare room to check the state of curtains, either wrinkled or lack thereof. I settled on *Magnum PI* because

Deb liked that rerun too. I dialed the railroad to check my stand number and found that I was two times out, the second engineer to be called for a train, and therefore would need to lay down for rest soon. After Deb and I watched Magnum and Angela Lansbury save the day I headed to bed. Deb stayed up reading. The 2100 hours bedtime was too early for her to finish up her day.

The phone blared and disturbed my rest once again. I answered, "Ben Time here."

The automated call informed me I was to be on the W654 at 0400. I set my alarm for 0300. I was pretty good at showering, grabbing my grip and my lunch, and pulling into the yard in one hour. Practice made perfect.

CHAPTER 3

INDIANAPOLIS, MARCH 19, 0400 EST

I pulled into the Indianapolis yard. The gray buildings looked drab in the man-made lighting. I wondered if the only color of paint that the railroad purchased was gray as I slid my bag out of the truck. As I entered the building I saw Lurch standing, no blocking, the doorway of the crew room. He couldn't help blocking it. I guessed his elongated frame would fill any doorframe.

"Hey, big guy," I said as I walked past the doorway toward the coffee pot.

He turned and said, "Hi Ben, I see we got this run together."

"Yeah, you're my favorite conductor. The dispatchers know it. Did you get the paperwork yet?" I asked.

"No, it seems the van-train is running late. So, you might just as well come in here and finish up your coffee.

The computers are down now and I'm sure they won't have the consist for the train ready for a while."

I hated waiting on late trains but it was often part of the job. The order of cars, the consist in railroad talk, is all done by computer now, so when they're down, so are we. I jabbed Lurch in the side and made my way into the crew room with my coffee, black, strong and overflowing a bit, as I walked.

I greeted the Mad Russian and his engineer Ty who were in deep complaint mode. "Hi, guys. What's got you two in a mood?" I asked.

"We were called in two hours ago. Still no paperwork and short on rest. You may have a wait too, Ben."

"I know. Lurch told me," I replied as I took a long sip of coffee. Lurch moved into the room and took a seat across the table from me and sipped at his java. Just then a new voice entered the crew room. Road foreman Ed Lawson glanced around the table and said we were a motley crew and should be moving trains. We looked up at the smiling face and all muttered, "Yeah, sure," "Wish we could," "Loved to," and the like. We kept unsightly language down because Ed was management. Ed wasn't the bad sort. He didn't enjoy pulling crews out of service. He ran a locomotive most of his working years and took the position of road foreman about five years ago when he was transferred here from Evansville.

As Ed sat down to join us a voice from the overhead speaker informed the Mad Russian that his paperwork was ready and he and Ty could get on their train coming down the main. They both stood and grabbed their grips and saluted us good bye or good riddance, never sure which, with those two.

Lurch said he was going to the train master's office to get an idea how long we would be waiting. He rose and followed our comrades out into the hallway.

Ed looked at me and said, "I hope it isn't me that caused the mass exodus, Ben."

"No, just good timing. How's everything going in your territory?" I asked.

"Getting more pressure to pull guys out of service for violations because of the derailment. If the dispatchers would have sent out a rail inspector the whole great mess wouldn't have happened. They always want to play the blame game instead of own up and solve the real problems. You guys take care running. All management will be under pressure to pull you trainmen out of service."

"Thanks for the heads-up. I appreciate the warning," I said as I gulped down the last of the caffeine and thought that Ed may know something about my last very quiet conductor who was also from Evansville.

"Hey Ed, do you know Rocko from Evansville? He just bumped up here about two months ago. He doesn't seem to want to open up much. Is he just quiet or what?"

"I do, or did, know Rocko. Best stay your distance, Ben. He got in some trouble involving a positive drug test. I think he went to counseling or rehab and spent eight months on the street, pulled out of service, but was placed back in service when rehab was finished up. When I was an engineer most of the other engineers didn't want to work with him. Some said he came on duty high most of the time. I ran with him only a couple of times. I don't know if he was on drugs or not but he didn't talk much. He may have bumped up here to get a new start as a drug free man or just get away from management who might have had his number."

"I know a lot of the guys come to you and ask some personal questions, Ben. They seem to trust you since you're the union chaplain and all. Can I ask you a question and ask that you keep it confidential?"

I responded, "Sure, Ed."

Ed looked me straight in the eyes and said, "As a management employee, we get undue pressure to pull guys out of service. Our jobs are threatened if we don't take the jobs of others. I was pulled out of service when I was an engineer. I know how it feels. No income, feeling like a failure, and forbidden to work. I don't want to set up the guys for failures, but I might lose my job if I don't. The pressure is that extreme."

"Can you bump back to locomotive engineer?" I asked.

"Only if I moved back to Evansville. My son is a senior here. I don't want to uproot my family again. Not now."

"How many years until you can get out?" I asked.

"I have seven more years and that's if I bump back to an engineer. I'll have to work longer if I remain in a management position."

The culture of the railroad was a harsh one. It pitted management against union employees. Some egos were fed by taking another man's job, his source of income, his only way to provide for his family. I could empathize with Ed. I lowered my eyes and asked Ed, "Can I pray with you?"

He nodded in the affirmative and I prayed.

"Dear heavenly Father, You are mighty, full of wisdom and love. You are our Creator and Redeemer. Thank you, Father, for your gifts of mercy, of grace, and of goodness. Father, we come to you asking for wisdom for Ed concerning his job. You know the pressure that he is under to be unjust and you know that this is not from you. Father, please give Ed wisdom to speak and act justly and courage to carry out your will. Let your will be done in this situation, Father and to you be the glory. Amen and Amen."

Just as I finished praying, Lurch entered with our paperwork and informed me that I was officially to place my big keester behind the controls of the W654.

I thanked Ed again for the warning and picked up my grip, threw my coffee cup in the trash, and walked through the yard office door.

Lurch asked me about the warning I had mentioned to Ed as we walked to the fuel pad to get our train. I relayed the information that management was under pressure to pull us lowly trainmen out of service. We were to be the scapegoats for the derailment, I added as I threw my grip up onto the engine. After Lurch threw his grip into the engine, we took our seats. I notified the dispatcher we were ready to leave. He gave permission for us to be on our way. I took the controls and watched as the yard lights slowly dim behind us.

CHAPTER 4

INDIANAPOLIS, MARCH 19, 0600 EST

"Two hours behind schedule," I said as I pulled the throttle and glanced down at the computer screens. I had two screens below the elongated front window to observe the connectivity of the train, the air pressure in the hoses, speed and more. Behind me were numerous electronic lights and switches. These new engines resembled the cockpits of airplanes. A far cry from the engines of old that contained a few levers.

"They'll want this train to get through, Ben. We'll get the signals to fly."

"Then fly we will, but not over the speed limits. I want to keep my job."

We saw our first clear signal and I began to accelerate. It was still dark and foggy. Just as we were approaching the haunted bridge I spotted a shadow that appeared to be leaning over the railing and suddenly seemed to drop into the darkness below. The fog was heavy over the bridge because the water temperature below was very cold this early spring morning. I asked Lurch if he had seen anything. He responded that he thought he had seen someone drop over the railing like a misty apparition. He rubbed his eyes trying to clear his vision.

"I think I better report this to the train dispatcher." I called the dispatcher and told him what we saw. He asked if we hit anything. I told him, "No. Nothing was on the rails. The figure we saw was on the walkway of the bridge at least a hundred feet ahead of us."

He said he would report the sighting to the town authorities and informed us to keep our train moving west.

We obeyed and kept moving. Lurch and I discussed the shadowy figure well into our trip. We knew that it could have been a teenage prank or someone could have jumped into the creek below or missed and hit the road that also ran under this particular bridge. Neither of us was sure of where on the bridge, over water or over road, the incident had occurred. Our confusion resulted from an incident that was unexpected, we were moving, and it was dimly lit, and shrouded in fog. We weren't even sure if it happened at all. We just hoped it wasn't a life-threatening incident.

I mentioned that just the day before I had discussed the haunted bridge with Betty. She had asked about it. I relayed the three ghost stories I found online again to Lurch and commented on their sadness.

Lurch asked, "You don't think there is anything to them, do you, Ben?"

I responded, "Nah," but was beginning to wonder a bit. "I'll call the dispatcher toward the end of our run and see if he knows anything more about the incident."

The rest of the trip went by smoothly. We watched as the night turned from black to gray and finally, to robin's egg blue. With the sun behind us, the morning appeared to slowly unfold as if the Lord Himself were pulling up the shade. We received permission to enter the yard in the full brightness of day and yarded the train without incident. I had called our IW dispatcher before our last clear signal to see if he knew anything about our shadowy figure in the dark of early morning, and he said he hadn't heard a thing. Lurch and I were disappointed but knew that local authorities rarely reported back to dispatchers. We decided to pursue the incident further when we returned to Indianapolis.

After Lurch finished up our time slips, Chuck picked us up in the yard in the minivan. We were both ready for sleep once we arrived at the hotel. When I reached my room, it took only minutes to crash. I slept hard. It seemed as if I were dead to the world only seconds when I slowly opened my eyes. I shook my head to get rid of the remainder of sleep and rose to peek out the large window in the room. It was dark so I pulled the drape open and looked at the room clock in the dim light. It was 2100 hours. My stomach indicated it was overdue for a meal. I showered, dressed, and thought I might be lucky and run into Lurch in the foyer. It was quiet when

I reached the front desk so I grabbed a cup of coffee and a cookie and asked Sherry, the other front desk clerk who shared the late-night hours with Amy, if she had seen Lurch. Just as she began to indicate she had not, Lurch appeared, startling us both. He was usually an early riser but had slept today.

"Speak of the devil," Sherry said as she tipped her head back to see Lurch's blue eyes just a few inches from the hanging light fixture above the front desk.

Lurch greeted us both and asked if I wanted to walk over to all-night restaurant across the parking lot from the hotel.

I responded, "Thought you'd never ask."

We waved to Sherry and walked through the sliding glass doors. Once at the restaurant we were seated in a booth, served coffee, and ordered two complete breakfasts.

"I hope we learn more about the ghostly figure we saw on the bridge, Ben."

We talked on this matter for a while then I thought I'd ask Lurch if he had any insight into Rocko. He said that he really didn't since they didn't work together, both being conductors. But he knew that Sudsy wasn't handling being bumped off this Saint Louis pool well. Sudsy had bumped onto the extra board but hated the cut he would be taking in pay while on that board. A pool job was more consistent in runs and pay than the extra board was. I told Lurch what I saw when Rocko and I both got out of the minivan from our return trip. I expounded about Rocko and Sudsy going at it in the parking lot. Just as I finished my story my phone went off alerting us both by the "Don't worry, Be Happy" ringtone that it was our call for the return trip home. I responded to the human voice that I was with Lurch and would give him the details of the trip.

"We're on the E178 at 2400 EST," I said.

"The midnight train to Indiana," Lurch said as he put two sugars in his coffee and chuckled at his own quip.

We had some time to kill before the railroad limo would be in the front of the hotel to pick us up so we sat and talked about life other than the railroad. I discovered that Lurch was still dating Kim. It had been nearly eight months of dating and they were quite serious. Kim had lasted longer than most of Lurch's romances. Lurch informed me that she had recently found a church to attend. Maybe she would be a good influence on this elongated trainman. We finished up breakfast and coffee, tipped our waitress, and walked over to the hotel to get packed for the return trip.

CHAPTER 5

SAINT LOUIS, MARCH 19, 2400 EST

I arrived at the minivan first, placed my bag in the rear, proceeded to the front passenger seat, and sat beside Norm. "How you doing, buddy?" I asked.

Norm said, "Doing fine, Big Ben, Just fine. How about you?"

I responded, "Couldn't be better if I were dancing a jig."

Just then the backseat door was opened and a grip flew in. Lurch had arrived. He greeted Norm as well. We buckled up and I asked if Norm would make a quick stop at the sub shop for us to pick up a lunch for the trip home. I use the term, "lunch" loosely because it could be any meal at any time. Norm nodded in the affirmative and off we went.

At the sub shop, I got my favorite ham and cheese and a chicken teriyaki for Lurch. I completed the meals with oatmeal cookies and baked chips to save a few calories. When I returned to the limo Norm and Lurch were ending a rather loud discussion concerning the recent road construction in downtown Saint Louis. I was glad I returned at the end of the discussion. We continued on to the railyard. Lurch went in search of our paperwork and I talked with the new, or fairly new train master, John. John took George the Tyrant's place last fall when George met his untimely demise from a whack on the head from a spike maul. George no longer controlled the trains. This delighted most of the trainmen since George took great joy from making us wait unusually long periods of time to begin our return trips home, and he loved to flaunt his power. John, on the other hand, was a young guy just out of college and trying to figure out the harsh culture of railroad work. He was freshly scrubbed and dressed in a polo shirt and khaki pants. He didn't yet resemble those who worked long hours in the bleakness of a railroad yard office. I hoped to befriend him before the culture changed him. We talked about the Saint Louis Cardinals and his hopes for a good season.

Lurch appeared and greeted John and told me that Norm would get us to our train. We got back into the waiting limo and Norm drove us to the E178 within ten minutes. We relieved a thankful crew from a foreign railroad and left for home.

Our trip home was in the black of night and without incident. We got a clear signal into the yard. However, the Indianapolis yardmaster radioed us and said he would like to see us when we got our train put away. I wondered what was up. I was somewhat concerned because Ed Lawson gave us heads-up that someone may be pulled out of service. Having to report to a yardmaster is never welcome news. I glanced over at Lurch and saw his brow creased as well. We brought the ponies to the diesel house tracks, tied them down, and debarked from the train for the yard office. Lurch went to the computer and I went to the yardmaster's office.

"Hi Tom, you wanted to see us? Lurch will be here in a minute. He's putting in our time slip."

"There's a nurse around the corner, standing in front of the health coordinator's office. The two of you need to drug test."

"OK, we'll do," I responded, relieved this meeting was not about any violation, made up or real.

I walked around the corner and met the nurse. She asked if I was familiar with the routine and I responded in the affirmative, took my plastic cup with my name printed on it and proceeded to the restroom. Random drug-testing has been part of railroad life since 1987 when an Amtrak train collided with light power consisting of three Conrail locomotives that failed to stop at an interlocking signal northeast of Baltimore. It was a horrible accident. The Amtrak train was traveling at 108 miles per hour. Sixteen were killed and 164 other people on the trains were injured. The Conrail engineer and his conductor had shared a joint as they left the railyard. The crew had failed to stop at the interlocking. The Conrail conductor served time in jail, the Conrail engineer served four years in a Maryland prison for his role in the accident. The Amtrak engineer was one of the sixteen killed. The FRA implemented drug testing for trainmen and Congress later implemented drug testing for all "safety sensitive" workers that are regulated by the US Department of Transportation.

I returned my cup to the nurse just as Lurch was getting his cup. Alcohol was once the poison of choice of trainmen. Now it seemed to be drugs. I see the wisdom in random drug testing. We needed to be at our best while operating a locomotive at fifty to sixty miles per hour. Some guys still take chances and break the rules, though. I stopped to speak to Karen, the Health Coordinator. Her office was located just beyond the crew room and she was often in a position to hear the guys and their unsavory talk. She was a nice young woman, about the age of my oldest daughter. She had been college educated and was employed here to help us maintain our health. She put up with sleazy talk and some of the guys trying too hard just to gain her attention as best she could.

"Hey, Miss Karen, how's your day going?" I asked as I stuck my head into her office.

"Good, Ben. Are you leaving for a trip or just getting back?" she asked.

"I'm just getting back."

"Do you have time for a work out? That's why we installed that gym next door."

"Not this morning but I've been trying to use the fitness room over at the hotel. I'm taking your advice and trying to get a mile of walking in every other day.

It seems impossible to get the mile in every day with no work schedule. Nights and days all mix together."

"Just keep trying. I want to see you stay with us a while longer. I can't say the same for all the guys. Don't tell anyone I said that."

"It's just between you and me. Have a good one." I turned to see Lurch handing the nurse his cup.

"Hey, Ben, did you find out anything more about the shadowy figure on the bridge?"

"You know, I completely forgot to ask. I think I'll go back to Tom's office and see if he knows anything."

I walked around the corner and knocked on Tom's door frame. He turned in his chair and asked what I wanted in a most unwelcoming voice. He was a heavyset man who looked as if he always needed a shave. Tom rarely, if ever, smiled. As he rotated on his chair I said, "Tom, Lurch and I reported seeing someone appearing to go over the railing of the haunted bridge the other morning. Have you heard anything about it from the town authorities?"

"Oh, I almost forgot since the nurse was here. The authorities want to talk to you and Lurch. They'll be contacting you both. That's all I know Ben." He turned to answer his phone.

I walked to the crew room told Lurch what I'd been told and exited the yard office to get home.

CHAPTER 6

RETURNED TO INDIANAPOLIS, MARCH 20, 1030 EST

checked my watch on the way home and figured that Deb would be upstairs working on an education project for the college. She worked from home most spring semesters. Rather than call and disturb her train of thought I decided I would just surprise her with my presence. I pulled in our driveway, opened the garage door, and took off my work boots in the garage. Since the garage was under the upstairs bonus room, Deb's workroom, I knew the sound of the garage door opening would alert her that I had returned.

I hollered upstairs, "Hey, Deb, your best-looking boyfriend is home."

"I'm sure glad it's the best-looking one," she replied.

"I don't want to disturb your work so I'm going to watch TV for a while," I said as I walked toward our bedroom.

If she replied I didn't hear it. Betty was right that most trainmen are hard of hearing. I changed into shorts and a T-shirt, my sleepwear, and walked back out into the kitchen searching for a snack.

Deb has hearing like a jackrabbit and yelled down, "Stay away from the cake. I baked it for the Housefields. John just returned from having back surgery."

I huffed loudly and opened the refrigerator door. I found a left-over brat and some Diet 7-up. After heating the brat in the microwave and adding mustard I took my plate and cup into the family room. I turned on the TV and found one of my favorite reruns of *Gunsmoke*. Matt Dillon always got his man. It's something I counted on. I just finished eating my brat when the cell phone rang. I looked down and saw that I would be speaking to law enforcement.

"Good morning," I answered after pushing the correct button on the phone.

The male voice on the other end replied, "Good morning. Is this Ben Time?"

"Yes, it is." I replied.

"This is the Avon Police Department, I am Detective Robert Holman calling to ask some questions concerning your reported sighting on the railroad bridge that crosses State Route 625 on March nineteenth. Could you go over the details of what you saw on the bridge, Mr. Time."

I went over the facts in a matter of a minute since there were so few. Then I asked the detective if they found anything. He responded that about a mile south of the bridge in the White Lick Creek they found a body of a male probably in his forties. He was unsure as to how long the body was there. It had been caught in the root system of a fallen tree. The creek had been unusually high and running quickly for the past two weeks due to spring rains and previous snow melt. There was a bullet hole in the body but they were waiting on a forensic report as to cause of death. He was unsure if the body had anything to do with what Lurch and I saw on the haunted bridge. He thanked me for my information which was sparse and stated that he would contact Lurch as well. I hung up and thought some moments about the body and about our shadowy figure going over the side of the bridge.

I watched the next rerun, *Bonanza,* and began to get sleepy. I got up and hollered up to Deb that I was going in for my beauty rest. She said I didn't have that much time for true improvement, so she would wake me at 6:30 and we could go for dinner.

I replied, "See you then. I will be a whole new man you'll see." And walked into my pad.

Deb came in and woke me by opening the black-out drapes and telling me that I sure did look like a whole new man. I couldn't believe it was 6:30 already. Seemed like three minutes had passed. I showered and dressed and was still groggy but ready for a meal. I asked Deb if she had finished up her project and she replied that she had and emailed it to work. During my beauty rest she also had time to deliver the cake to the Housefields. She recounted that John was feeling some better now that he was home. We put on our jackets and began our drive to meet our friends, the Reeds, for dinner.

Deb said, "We'll be eating at Stoneys Too. I'll miss the Housefields, they can't join us tonight because John has a way to go in his recovery. I suppose Ron will be his usual witty self and Linda has a nose for news. It's great to have such entertaining friends. I look forward to our dinners together."

We arrived at the restaurant, got our seats, and began our usual talk of the week's events. Linda asked if we had seen the evening news. We both shook our heads in the negative. She said they found a body under the railroad bridge in Danville. The body was still unidentified and may be related in some way to the body they found in White Lick Creek in Avon. She added that everything was still under investigation.

Linda asked, "Did you hear anything about this Ben, on the railroad, since it involves the railroad bridges?"

All eyes turned to me. I felt like E.F. Hutton. "Well, Lurch and I saw a ghostly apparition on the haunted bridge while heading to Saint Louis on our last trip. The body seemed to go over the side of the bridge." I explained the follow up call from the Avon police. I told both Ron and Linda that this was the first I had heard about a second body being discovered under the Danville bridge.

"That is very unusual to find two bodies just five miles from one another," I commented.

Ron suggested that I investigate the bodies since I had some luck in uncovering the murderer of George the Tyrant last fall. I thought he was teasing, as usual, and took a long sip of ice tea.

We stopped our talking of bodies and had an enjoyable dinner then left for home.

I asked Deb if she wouldn't mind driving home since I was getting sleepy once again. She didn't mind and off we went.

She asked, "What do you think about the two bodies, Ben? Do you think they're related in some way in death or life? I sure hate the increase in violence I've seen in my lifetime," she added.

"I hate the violence too. I don't know if there's a relationship between the two or not. But, I'll be paying some attention to the investigation. It's too close to home."

We quieted for the rest of the trip, both of us deep in thought about a world that seemed to be, damaged, hurting, angry, and increasingly violent.

When we got home I went back to sleep to get a few more hours of rest before the next trip. Deb said she was going to stay up and watch the news. I guessed the fact that the two bodies that were found nearly in our own back yard since we lived in Danville, and the bridge is just a mile down the road, concerned her. I too was concerned about Deb's security. I wasn't home to see to it nearly often enough.

Violence occurred too often and we seemed helpless to stop it. I was thinking that we, as a society, were just getting kind of numb to it; a very disconcerting thought, numbness to loss of human life, life made in the very image of God, hardening of our hearts. I prayed for God to have mercy on us all and to give me wisdom concerning the ever hardening of hearts, my own heart, and all hearts of others.

CHAPTER 7

INDIANAPOLIS, MARCH 21, 0300 EST

I received my wakeup call at 0100 and was told to be on the W103X train with Jonsey as my conductor at 0300. Deb was sleeping through the intrusion of the ring in the night. She often did. I guess years of phone calls in the night has trained her up to ignore the blast. I showered, packed, and decided I would stop at McDonalds to pick up my lunch. I pulled into the yard in the rain. It was a light rain, not torrential, so I gathered my grip and lunch, and walked rapidly to the office. Jonsey was getting the paperwork.

"Hi Ben, we'll be ready to leave momentarily, all the paperwork is ready. We have a Federal Marshal riding with us tonight. Did you notice the X at the end of the 103 call letters?"

"I did. Wonder what the freight is tonight?" I asked as I walked toward my locker, not really expecting an answer. The extra call letter, the X, meant that the freight needed a government guard. This always made me just a bit jittery. The marshal rode in the second engine and rarely spoke to us trainmen. I finished getting my waterproof jacket from my locker, turned, and saw Jeff Longpaw slamming his locker door. Jeff was of Native American descent so we called him Indian. We trainmen were not politically correct with nicknames. Jeff was about six feet tall with coal black eyes and long hair to match. I was a bit jealous of his hair amount since mine resembled a recently deforested hillside.

"Hi, Indian, rough night?" I asked.

"Yep. I think MR and I will be pulled out of service as soon as they look over our speed tapes," he said as he punched the locker.

This was not the time for a conversation. Indian needed some time to cool down. So, I turned and said that I hoped that would not be the case and left the locker room. I followed Jonsey out to the fuel pad. We observed the US Marshal crawl up into the second engine and give us a wave. We received permission from the train dispatcher and the yardmaster to move and I throttled up.

Jonsey and I paid attention to business for a while then began to talk. After I crossed the haunted bridge and was nearing the Danville bridge I asked Jonsey, "Have you heard about the two bodies discovered, one under each bridge…well, rather, one under a bridge and the other down creek."

He replied, "I hadn't heard anything about it but hadn't watched the news in a few days. I was called out earlier then I had guessed because the new guy on the board, Rocko, had not taken his call. You know Ben, that's not good to be missing calls when you're the new guy."

"That's for sure. If he misses another he'll lose his job and he better have a very good excuse for this time. I worked with him the trip before last. He didn't want to talk but did his job okay."

"Don't know much about him but I do know that Sudsy isn't taking being bumped from the Saint Louis pool well. But if Rocko messes up on taking calls, Sudsy will get his spot on this board back," Jonsey added.

Because we were on a government protected train we got signals to keep it moving. The freight made me a bit nervous. It was sometimes referred to by the guys as the glowworm train one carrying nuclear waste, but it may not be a glowworm. We weren't privy to that information. However, we were moving speedily on toward Saint Louis. It would be a fast trip. Jonsey called the signals. There were signals along the tracks every two miles. They were red, green, and yellow just like traffic signals. The conductor's job was to call the signal by stating "stop, clear, or approach." This was an extra warning to correct speed for the engineer. Because we had clear signals and didn't stop the train we just barely had time to gobble up our lunches. We made it to the yard in six hours and twenty minutes, a good run. The marshal jumped down from the engine and said, "Good run, boys!" and walked toward the yard office.

We jumped down and followed suit. Jonsey took care of the paperwork and we went out to get in the limo for our ride to the hotel. Betty was leaning against the minivan putting out her cigarette.

"Hi guys," she said as she tossed the butt on the grass at the edge of the parking lot.

"Hey, Betty, how's it going this beautiful morning?"

"Good, Ben. It is a nice morning. Spotted a robin right away."

"It was raining back in Indianapolis but it's nice to see the sun and feel its warmth today," I replied, as we rode to the hotel.

Jonsey said he wasn't tired yet and asked if I wanted to go out for breakfast. I told him I was tired and always ready for rest and would catch a meal with him before we left for our return trip.

I checked in with the front desk. Sherry was on duty and said I had a message as she handed me a slip of paper. I thanked her, got my cookie, and went up to my room. I threw my grip on the bathroom counter top and headed toward the red and blue stripped overstuffed chair. I stopped and opened the curtains for light, sat down, and unfolded my message.

Mr. Time,

Can you give me a call as soon as possible? My phone number is 317-505-0555.

Detective Robert Holman

I thought that his message was certainly to the point, no excess verbiage at all. I touched the proper numbers and detective Robert Holman picked up on the first ring.

"Detective Holman, this is Ben Time returning your call. What can I do for you?" I asked.

"Hi, Mr. Time, I wanted to let you know that we identified the body in White Lick Creek. It was that of James Rice, also known as Rocko. After checking with the railroad, I found that you have worked with him. I hope this news isn't too much of a shock for you, but it seemed that no one in the Indianapolis yard knew much about him. Since we have already spoken I was hoping you could tell me more about the man."

That did take me aback. I sat stunned for a moment then replied, "I am shocked, not even sure what to say. I worked with Rocko just a few days ago. I'm afraid I don't know much about him, though. Rocko just recently began working this pool. That's why no one in Indianapolis seems to know much about him. He bumped up here from Evansville. The trip I worked with him was our first and only trip together. I did try and talk with him but he was very reluctant to open up. His silence may have been because he was new to our pool. Some of the old-timers give the new guys a hard time and he may have been suspicious that I would give him a hard time as well. I had thought maybe he would talk more on the return trip. We got a deadhead home so it was in a minivan. He was basically silent," I added.

"Is there anything you can think of that was unusual about the man? Did he seem afraid, nervous or angry?"

"Only his reluctance to talk. I guess I'm a talker so his silence seemed a bit strange to me. You know, on our ride home our van driver, Betty, asked me what I knew about the haunted bridge. I told her what I knew from the town's website. So Rocko would have heard the information just the day before his death. I don't know if he knew about the bridge before the conversation since he was relatively new to this area. It just seems strange he was found near the bridge just after my conversation with Betty."

"Why would this Betty want to know more about the bridge?"

"I don't know. She may have heard the guys talking about the bridge on other runs and was just curious. I don't know," I mumbled out the second time.

"How can I get in touch with Betty?" the detective asked.

I gave him the limo company phone number then thought to ask, "Did you identify the body under the Danville bridge?" I asked slightly concerned that I might know the identity of the man who lost his life.

"Yes, the Danville police department have identified him as Richard Hines, also employed by the railroad, as a dispatcher. Did you know him by any chance, Mr. Time?"

"No, I'm afraid not. He must not have been dispatching the west bound trains. Did he work from downtown Indianapolis?" I asked.

"Yes, The Danville police are investigating this one but we are conferring on the two cases. I believe since they were both railroad employees the railroad police department will be called in as well. Is there any additional information you can think of, Mr. Time, that may help solve this crime? It is definitely a crime because the cause of death for Rocko was the gunshot wound in his back. We are not yet sure if there is a crime concerning Richard Hines. There was no gunshot wound on his body and forensics is still attempting to discern the cause of death."

"I can't think of any additional information right now, Detective. But if anything comes to mind, I'll give you a call."

"Thanks, Ben. You have my number. Let me know if you think of anything more."

I took note that Detective Holman and I were now on first name basis. I did like the young man's phone demeanor. He was polite, efficient, and thoughtful. I rested my head on the back of the overstuffed chair and placed my phone on the desk. I could hardly digest the fact that the man I worked with just a few days ago was now dead from a gunshot wound. It was just so very hard to believe. In addition, hard to believe that another railroad man, a crew dispatcher, was dead. A dispatcher had no reason to be out on the tracks, on a bridge or under it in the dark of early morning. This was all very peculiar. I was rapidly sinking into a stupor. I dragged myself up to wash my face and get ready for sleep. I would have to think on this later.

CHAPTER 8

SAINT LOUIS,
MARCH 21, 1800 EST

woke up without the aid of a phone blaring. I hadn't slept well. I tossed and turned and dreamt of Rocko sinking into a lake, slowly, silently, and I could not get to him to help. The fear of his drowning woke me. I was breathing hard and was shaking. It took only moments for me to remember the truth of the situation. The thoughts were not comforting at all. I rose and showered, attempting to wake fully and remove, by washing, the frightful shadow that seemed to encompass me. I pulled on my blue jeans, T-shirt and flannel shirt and left my room behind.

Once I reached the hotel lobby I spotted Steve at the front desk.

"Hey Steve, I haven't seen you in while. I guess I've been missing your shifts. How's it going?"

Steve responded, "Not bad, Ben. Things have been pretty normal here. We had a tornado watch last week. That always gets the customers excited. Were you here then?"

"No, missed the excitement. I was home in Indianapolis getting my beauty sleep."

"Must have missed a few Z's." Steve laughed at his own reply.

I poured myself a cup of coffee and grabbed a cookie from the glass enclosed case, ignoring Steve's sense of humor. I asked if he had seen Jonsey.

"Haven't seen him yet tonight."

I heard the ding of the elevator door opening as Steve responded and just on cue Jonsey appeared.

Steve said, "Speak of the devil."

"Good timing, Jonsey. Are you ready for dinner?" I asked.

"It looks as if you already started," Jonsey replied as he looked over at my half-eaten cookie. "My mother says I'm an angel, front desk boy!" he added to Steve.

Steve looked sheepishly down at his I-pad and mumbled, "Well, you did show up on cue."

I gulped my coffee and swallowed the last of cookie and asked Jonsey where he would like to go for dinner.

He responded, "Rondinellies."

I said "Let's go get the car and we'll be off." We left through the front doors of the hotel walked around back to the rust bucket that four of us shared custody. We had gotten permission from the hotel to keep it parked in the back so as not to embarrass the proprietors. Keeping the old jalopy allowed us some freedom off premises. Sometimes we were stuck here for several days.

Jonsey and I pulled into Rondinellies. It was busy as usual for this time of evening. We waited several minutes until we were seated near the salad bar, always my favorite place to be seated. We filled our plates with healthy choices first. I would return for the dessert bar to upset my good choices later. Between bites I filled Jonsey in on what I knew of the body found near the haunted bridge. He was also very surprised that the body was that of Rocko. Jonsey asked, "What do you think Rocko was doing out there?"

"I have no idea," I replied.

"Do you know how they identified him?"

"I don't know. It was a fairly quick identification of both bodies." Then I told Jonsey about the second body being that of a dispatcher from downtown named Richard Hines. "Did you know him?"

Jonsey said he had never heard of him and also added that the dispatcher must not have been assigned to the west bound trains. Then after a short pause Jonsey said, "This is very strange, Ben. Very strange indeed."

I told Jonsey that Lurch and I had spotted a shadowy figure going over the rail of the haunted bridge approximately the same time Rocko would have been shot. I was very suspicious that the shadowy figure we had seen that foggy early morning was Rocko. Detective Holman did not indicate on the phone it was Rocko but I was sure he was suspicious that it was indeed our late conductor.

I finished filling Jonsey in on all that I discovered through my conversation with Detective Holman and we finished with our main courses of broasted chicken, mashed potatoes, and green beans. It was now time for a trip to the dessert bar for both of us. I selected a slice of deep dish apple pie and added some vanilla ice cream from the self-serve machine. Jonsey selected double layer chocolate cake. He didn't dilute the chocolate with anything. He was a true chocoholic.

While eating our desserts we got our work calls for the return trip just moments apart from each other. The crew dispatcher was on the ball. We finished our meal and drove back to the hotel. I told Jonsey I would see him shortly on the van ride to the yard office. I went to my room turned on the TV and watched a half hour of *Columbo.* I would certainly not want to be on Columbo's list. He always got his man or woman and frustrated them terribly to boot. I gathered up the contents of my grip, turned off the TV, and left the room.

Chuck was waiting in the van outside the hotel sliding doors. I greeted him and got the front seat. Jonsey followed about two minutes later, threw his grip in the back and lunged in himself. Chuck was his same old chipper self and asked if we wanted to stop to pick up food. Both of us groaned and said "not tonight, Chuck" almost simultaneously. I guess the dessert did the trick. We were both full. Chuck got us safely to the yard office where we said our collective thanks and entered the dingy building at precisely 2200 hours EST. Jonsey went to get the paperwork I went to the coffee pot to get one last cup before our trip. Just as I finished filling the Styrofoam cup, Jonsey walked up behind me and said, "You better settle in for a few. The paperwork isn't ready." I asked if he knew how late our train might be and he shook his head. I added the packet of creamer to my coffee and walked into the crew room. Jonsey followed suite and sauntered into the crew room. I texted my wife that I would probably be home sometime tomorrow morning.

Jonsey looked over and asked, "Do you think that there's anything to the haunted bridge thing?"

"Have you ever heard some moaning or seen anything when you've crossed?"

"No, but you saw something go over the side."

"I don't think it was a ghost."

"It may be one now, Ben. It may be one now…" he repeated.

"I think I'm going to take some time and write down some facts, some notes about all this in my phone since we're just waiting for the train to arrive."

I looked down at my phone opened up the notes app and began a list of facts. Jonsey sat and played Sudoku on his phone.

FACTS and QUESTIONS

1. Body found in White Lick Creek was that of Rocko, James Rice.
2. Saw figure go over side of haunted bridge on March 19 approximately 0600 EST. Was the figure that of Rocko?

3. Cause of death was gunshot wound in back. Need to find out how they identified the body so quickly.

4. Why was Rocko out on the bridge the day after we discussed it in van?

5. Rocko missed a work call. Need to find out time and date. I think it was due to his death, but not sure?

6. Body found under bridge in Danville. It was that of dispatcher Richard Hines. Need to find out time and cause of death. Why was a crew dispatcher out on train bridge or under it in the early morning?

7. What was cause of death of crew dispatcher?

8. Did Rocko and crew dispatcher know one another?

That was all I could think of for the moment. I noticed that once again I had more questions than known facts listed.

While I was looking over the list the yardmaster came in and announced that our train was in and we could get the work orders momentarily from the computer. He turned and left rather abruptly. Jonsey hopped up and went to the computer. I glanced at my watch and noticed we had been in the crew room two hours and twenty minutes. For once when just waiting, time went by very quickly. I got up with my usual groan and hobbled toward the computer. Jonsey had our paperwork and we went out the door to relieve the inbound tired crew for our return trip home.

CHAPTER 9

SAINT LOUIS,
MARCH 22, 0130 EST

We received clearance to leave the yard. I slowly began to increase speed as Jonsey called out the clear signals. It was dark and rather cool out, probably just above freezing. I glanced behind us as the last of the yard lights disappeared into the blackness of night. I was anxious to get this trip behind us and be home. After several more clear signals the train dispatcher radioed and told us we would be pulling in the next siding. I needed to let an east bound train go by. We saw the approach signal as we pulled in. We waited, listening to the radio for the east bound train.

I hoped this would not be a trip of stops and sidings all night long. I had been expecting at least one more siding. That would be in Effingham where we would be picking up cars. We got clear signals all the way there. We stopped, picked up our cars, and began to move forward again. The dispatcher called and had us pull off into the very next siding, allowing another train to pass. I glanced at my watch and saw that we had been on duty for ten hours and ten minutes. I looked over at Jonsey and said, "We won't get this one into Indianapolis between starting out late and stopping at sidings all night long. We're in for a long run."

Dawn had already appeared, followed by a bright and beautiful morning. The scene was difficult on the eyes when traveling east into a blinding sun, the beginning of a new day. It was difficult and yet promising.

I slowed the train down and pulled us into the next siding. I was getting more tired in each passing minute and wished that we had picked up a sandwich before leaving on the trip. The broasted chicken was no longer holding me. I checked my grip for peanut butter crackers, my emergency rations. I had three packs. I thought that would hold me then thought of Jonsey. I offered him a pack and he was happy to join me. While eating I looked down the tracks and saw an animal of some kind. "What do you think that is?" I asked Jonsey as he sat, contented to munch down his crackers.

"I'm not sure," he responded. "But it's slowly making its way toward us."

We both stared out the windshield until we recognized, simultaneously, a rather large pink pig. It was walking right toward us. I said to Jonsey, "You better get out and chase that pink pig off the tracks. I'm not allowed to leave the engine." I laughed as I gave him my request.

"How do I chase a pink pig off the track? And did you notice he's about three hundred pounds?" he asked.

"Just get out and yell at him. The W234 will be past us soon and we will need to be on our way."

Jonsey reluctantly climbed down off the engine and started yelling, "Pig, pig, pig," in his most manly of voices I had noticed. The pink pig just stood and looked at him with the "I'm standing my ground" look. With Jonsey as a frame of reference I could now see that our pink friend was huge.

As man and pig faced each other in a standoff, the silence was suddenly broken by the roar of an engine. I hoped it was the cavalry. A farmer had pulled up on a four-wheeler. He looked over the situation and said, "Well, not my pig."

Jonsey spoke up. "How can you tell it's not your pig?"

The farmer responded, "The marks on his ear—not my marks," he said as he spat out a wad of chewing tobacco.

"Can you get him off the tracks?" Jonsey asked.

"Not my pig." The farmer started his engine, turned, and left Jonsey open-mouthed and hopping mad. So much for the cavalry.

I heard the W234 on the radio and decided I better let the train dispatcher know that our pink friend ambled over on to the main and would soon be pork chops if the W234 didn't slow down.

"This is the E133."

"Go ahead E133. This is the IW dispatcher."

"There's a large pink pig on the main in front of us and you might want to notify the W234 of the situation."

"What did you say, E133?" the IW train dispatcher asked.

"Pink pig on the track. Maybe you can get sheriff's department to move him. A farmer stopped and said he wasn't his pig. Jonsey has been yelling at the pig but he doesn't seem to speak pig well," I added to the train dispatcher.

I heard the train dispatcher call the W234 and slow him down. The Indian was at the handles. I recognized his voice. He must not have been pulled out of service. Good for him, I thought. The Indian was chuckling over the radio and said that he had been listening to the radio chatter and was slowing down. He added that he didn't care for ham salad. Just then our pink friend began to walk off the track and through the corn stubble. He headed up a slight rise in the barren field. Jonsey began climbing back on the engine and we watched the pig move up the hill and lie down under a lone tree. I called the dispatcher. "Pink pig is on the move, no need for sheriff and Indian can pass by."

"The dispatcher responded, "I got to get you and Jonsey home, Ben."

"Roger that, roger that," I responded.

We got back on course after the W234 passed and made it into Terre Haute just as we died, hitting our twelve-hour work shift limit. The dispatcher was as good as his word and had a van waiting for us and a new crew waiting to take the E133 into Indianapolis.

I slept the rest of the way in the minivan into the Indianapolis yard. I assumed that Jonsey did too. I awoke crossing the tracks into the yard, ending what seemed to be a dream about eating a great big ham dinner. Felt rather sorry it ended.

We had been on duty for thirteen and one-half hours. I was alert but looking forward to collapsing into sleep once I reached my home. I remembered that I had forgotten to text my wife and warn her of my impending arrival. When I entered the kitchen I yelled out, "Mertle, I'm home." The house was quiet. I looked at my watch and noted it was 1400 hours. I guess I did text her last night and told her to expect me home in the morning. I was late again. She left a note on the kitchen table.

I went up to Liz's house. We are cake decorating this afternoon. You may test the spoils when I get home.

Great! I thought as I dragged myself to the bedroom and collapsed.

CHAPTER 10

INDIANAPOLIS, MARCH 22, 2200 EST

I awoke slowly, feeling like I had been trampled by a heard of hippos. Deb was sleeping soundly, exhaling with a slight whistle. I wondered what time it was as I sneaked out of bed trying not to wake her.

I switched on the light in the family room and saw that it was 2200 hours. I wasn't sure yet what day of the week it was. I would have to check my time-book. I suddenly remembered the word "cake" and walked with anticipation to the kitchen. There it was. A two-layer cake, flavor unknown, but I could see the white butter cream frosting with various kinds of flowers covering its sides and top. It almost seemed a crime to cut it but I was starving. I cut a thick slice and saw that it was a marble cake then poured a glass of milk and sat down to enjoy the spoils.

The cake seemed to bring me back to life. I knew I had missed a meal or two because I was still hungry. I checked the refrigerator and saw that there was some leftover chicken noodle soup. Warmed the soup in two minutes, made a peanut butter and blackberry jam sandwich and was ready to retire to the recliner chair for nourishment and reruns.

I was fully alert now, remembered what day of the week it was; remembered the pink pig incident; and remembered that Rocko was deceased and so was a crew dispatcher. I glanced up at the TV. There was a rerun of *Gunsmoke*. It seemed to be about halfway through because Miss Kitty was once again warning Matt of impending danger. I wondered if Rocko had been warned of danger and decided to look over my notes in my phone.

I recalled that Rocko had been shot in the back. I wasn't sure if Rocko was the shadowy figure that went over the railing of the haunted bridge. I didn't know a thing about the dispatcher. I could make some calls tomorrow. Maybe Ed could give me some more information about Rocko or the dispatcher. He was formerly an Evansville man and he was in management so he may have been acquainted with the dispatcher. I watched the rest of *Gunsmoke* and an episode of the *Rifleman* then decided I could probably go back to sleep. I snuck into the bedroom without disturbing my wife and fell immediately back to sleep.

The next morning, I awoke early. It was still dark and I was the first to rise. I went to the kitchen to make some coffee, checked my stand number, noticed that I was one time out, next to get a train, then decided to fry up some eggs and toast two bagels. I might get some bonus points by serving breakfast. I usually needed them. I heard Deb in the shower and continued cooking. The eggs were a little hard but I was still hoping for the bonus points as I placed the plates on the table. Deb came out looking chipper. I knew I had received the bonus points as she surveyed the kitchen table.

She said, "Good morning. Missed you yesterday."

I replied that I would have to tell her my pink pig story as we both sat down and began to sip the coffee.

She added as she glanced at the counter, "I see you found the cake last night. How did you think it looked?"

"It tasted great! I may have another piece after breakfast. It looked almost too good to cut."

"I see you got over that thought." Deb rolled her eyes. "Liz and I practiced making our roses yesterday. I think she makes better ones than I do. Next week in cake decorating class we'll make pansies and two additional types of flowers. I can't seem to remember what type of flowers the instructor mentioned. Oh well. Now, what is the pink pig story?" She scooped up a bite of egg.

I regaled her with the pink pig incident as I finished my eggs and bagel. I rose and, as much as I shouldn't have, I cut another slice of cake and wolfed it down.

After we finished breakfast, Deb loaded the dishwasher as I walked into the bathroom to get my shower. I noticed as I passed by the front picture window it was an overcast morning. The kind that looked as if the clouds were soon going to shed buckets of spring rains. I showered and dressed just in time to pick up my phone. Railroad calling. The male voice announced his identity. He continued, "Is Mr. Time available?"

I responded, "This is he."

"Mr. Time, you are on the W431 at 0900 EST."

"Who is my conductor?" I asked.

"Mr. Evans," the dispatcher responded and hung up.

I walked out of the bedroom and into the kitchen. I told Deb that I needed to be on a train in two hours.

"I need to go into the college today and hand in my latest project so I'll be leaving as well. When do you think you'll be home for a day or so?" she asked.

I said, "I don't know, but if time off is for something important maybe I could arrange for a day off."

She said that it wasn't important but she would just like to do something together soon. And she added that she was getting a bit lonely.

Deb hadn't complained much about the lack of my presence or the lack of schedule but it had been a while since we have spent a whole day together. I would need to find a way to connect soon even if the railroad deemed otherwise.

We both left the house at the same time. I reached the railyard and began looking for Lurch. The conductors' board and the engineers' board are separate, so I never know, until the call, who I will work with. There are times I work with the same conductor three trips in a row and times I will work with a different conductor for each of fourteen trips. I was talking with Ty in the crew room when Lurch arrived with his baritone "Good morning," drawing out the word "morning" like the character, Lurch, in the *Adams Family.*

I greeted my favorite conductor with a "Hey."

Ty was exiting the crew room and gave us both a salute then warned Lurch to watch out that I was due to have a pork chop dinner soon one way or the other. Lurch looked at me and asked, "What did that mean?"

I responded that I would explain later and asked him if we had the paperwork for our trip. "We better get to the engine before the skies burst open."

He responded in the affirmative and we walked quickly to our locomotive. He no more wanted to walk the train in the rain than I would have. We both began our assigned duties and were ready to leave out. Lurch secured himself in his seat after his dry and rather hurried walk of the train. I received permission to leave the yard from the yard master and train dispatcher. I also began to recount the pink pig story. I followed up that story with what I knew about Rocko and the crew dispatcher, Richard Hines.

"Boy, Ben, do you ever have boring days?" he asked.

"Not lately." I replied. "Do you know the dispatcher, or have you heard anything about the man?"

"No, don't believe I do."

"I may just call Ed Lawson and see what he knows about both men when we get set out at the siding in Effingham. We'll be there for a while today." I looked out at the rain falling heavily enough to prepare the fields for the new crops of corn and soybeans.

Lurch looked over and said, "Better turn the wipers up a notch."

I glanced back over at him and asked, "Who's in the driver's seat, buddy?" as I turned the wipers up a notch.

It wasn't long before we reached the siding in Effingham. We decided to eat lunch while waiting. Lurch had an Italian sub and I had the ham sandwich, chips and an apple that Deb had left on the kitchen counter. No more cake for me, I noticed.

We would be here several hours at a standstill so I took out my phone and looked over my notes. I decided not to call Ed until I reached the hotel. I wouldn't want to put Ed in a position to pull me out of service for cell phone usage even though we were officially stopped for several hours. I read my notes to Lurch and asked if he could think of anything else.

He was quiet for a while then added, "I hate to say this but what was Sudsy doing at the time of Rocko's death? Was he on duty? And since Ed knew Rocko, what was he doing as well? I know you like them both but it may be worth finding out. What was the relationship between Rocko and the dispatcher?"

"All good questions. But, they are questions I don't really want to ask Ed and will be very careful if I do ask." I added Lurch's questions to my list.

The rain started to let up. The Indiana west dispatcher came on the radio and gave us permission to be on our way west.

"No pigs today, Ben." Lurch laughed as we pulled onto the main.

"I think that pig may have moved faster if he'd seen your six-foot seven-inch frame waving and yelling. Jonsey doesn't quite have the fierceness that you do."

"You bet your ham hocks he would have moved!" Lurch laughed again.

He always enjoyed his own humor, I thought, as we gained speed toward Saint Louis.

We got clear signals the rest of our trip and were permitted to enter the yard. On duty for eight hours and twenty minutes. Not a bad run considering the time spent in Effingham. Lurch and I were driven to the hotel by none other than Betty. I told her about Rocko and the dispatcher.

She said that it gave her the willies. "Ben, you know that Rocko was listening as we discussed the haunted bridge. Maybe it is a cursed bridge. What was he doing there?"

"I don't know, but the police detective on the case from Avon may call you, because you asked about the bridge the day before the murder."

"Boy! Ben, I just asked because I heard other guys talk about the bridge and we had just passed it on our trip."

"Don't worry," I told her. "That's all you have to say. The truth."

"You don't think they would suspect me? Like they suspected Chuck when George was murdered? Do you, Ben? Chuck was just waiting there at the yard to pick up his crew. That incident really stressed him out at a time when he didn't need any additional stress. I don't need the stress either."

"Don't worry, just the truth. Remember—just the truth- Do you have an alibi for March the...let me look up the date in my time-book." As I looked for the date Betty stopped our van in front of the hotel. Lurch, who appeared to be sleeping as Betty and I conversed, came back to life, got out, and said he would see me in the morning for breakfast. I looked for the date. "It was March nineteenth, maybe around 0600 EST? At least, that's when we saw the figure go over the bridge."

Betty looked in her time-book. "I was home sleeping. I guess that isn't the best of alibis."

"Well, remember, the truth will set you free." I got out of the van. Then I looked down at Betty and felt bad that I answered with a quote. "Don't worry, Betty. It will turn out okay. Call if you need me."

I walked into the hotel, got my room assignment, and headed to the elevator. I decided peanut butter crackers in my room would have to do for supper. I was more tired than I realized. Also, my call to Ed would have to wait until morning. I was too tired to think it through carefully. I laid down to put the day behind me at 2000 hours EST. It was dark and I was exhausted.

CHAPTER 11

SAINT LOUIS,
MARCH 24,
WOKE AT 0700 EST

woke at a normal waking hour, 0700. I peeked through the curtains and saw that it was still dark outside. I was rested enough to make a small pot of coffee in the room and turn on the TV. The news began with the local violence, two men found shot to death on the north side. A gas station robbed on the south side of town. I turned the television off. I decided a shower was needed to wash my body clean as well as my mind and spirit after listening to just five minutes of news.

I finished dressing and sat in the striped chair with coffee in hand and then tapped the Bible app on my phone to investigate the daily scripture. "For we are his workmanship, created in Christ Jesus for good works, which God afore prepared that we should walk in them" (Ephesians 2:10 ASV). I found that God's Word had a way of reminding me who was really in charge in this world and what I should be doing with my life. After some coffee and some minutes with the Lord I was prepared to meet the world head on.

I descended to the lobby and glanced into the restaurant. Lurch was already seated and sipping at his morning orange juice.

"Hi, Lurch. You're up and ready early." I startled him from his deep thinking as he jerked around to see who was speaking to him.

"Yep. There was a lot of commotion in the room next to mine this morning. Sounded like a herd of water buffaloes packing for an early departure. So, I showered, dressed, and made it to the one place I knew you would migrate to."

"I wasn't sleeping very well, anyway, over-thinking about what happened to Rocko. You know me," I said as I looked over the menu. The waitress took our orders and poured me some coffee.

"That really could have been Rocko going over the side of the bridge that morning. I just can't believe it. Why would he be out there early in the dark of morning? Why would a crew dispatcher be out on the Danville bridge or just near the bridge? Have you called Ed yet or found out any additional information?"

"No, I was too tired to ask the proper questions last night. I'll call this morning after breakfast."

"Okay, keep me posted."

I needed to change the subject from the macabre. "How are you and Kim coming along?"

"She got a promotion at work so she has longer hours. We aren't able to get many dates in now between her schedule and my lack of schedule. I miss her and she says she misses me. I hope she doesn't find someone else at work. I'm getting a little paranoid that there may be someone else. But I think it's just paranoia."

"Probably. Who could outshine you, buddy?" I asked as I slathered my toast with strawberry jam. Then added, "But to be sure, maybe send her some flowers."

We continued with some happier talk between bites of breakfast. As I finished up I told Lurch I was going to my room to make some phone calls. He said he was going to the fitness center to look good for Kim.

I got to my room and opened the curtains to let in the light of the morning. Dew glistened on the grass and the sky was an indigo blue. This would make for a nice trip home if we would get called out sooner than later I thought as I packed my grip. After packing I sat on the red and blue chair and looked over my phone notes so I could decide on the questions I would ask Ed.

I dialed Ed's number and to my surprise he picked up on the second ring. "Hey, Big Ben, what's wrong?"

"Nothing is wrong, Ed. What makes you ask?"

"I only get calls from hoggers when something is a dire emergency or they want to get out of trouble."

"Are you referring to us engineers?"

"I am, indeed. You know the slang for engineers is hoggers."

"I'm not in trouble, but you are the first one I would call if I were."

"Take me off that list, Ben." He laughed.

I thought, good, he's in a good mood. So, I proceeded with my questions.

"I have a few questions for you. You've probably heard about Rocko's death and that they found the body of a crew dispatcher named Richard Hines, dead under the Danville bridge."

"I have heard."

"What more do you know about Rocko?" I asked. "The first time I asked you it was just to get a feeling about his character because he was so quiet on our trip. But now he's dead, possibly the body I saw go over the side of the bridge the morning of the nineteenth. I reported it to the train dispatcher and was given permission to keep on moving."

"I don't know too much about the man. Like I said, it was rumored he had a drug problem. I think he came to Indianapolis after he had treatment for his addiction and served his eight months out of service. Possibly for a new start. I can check his record. I'll know for sure if he was treated and let you know. Don't they tell addicts to change environments to get away from friends or family that may have encouraged the problem? He was divorced. No kids. I ran into him one day at the yard office and he didn't speak, but I know he had recognized me."

"Did you know Richard Hines the crew dispatcher?"

"I knew his voice. When I was running on the Evansville pool I was being dispatched by Richard. He was a straight-to-the-point, no nonsense dispatcher and really resented any questions of his assignments. I didn't care for the man. He also had his favorites on the pool who seemed to mysteriously get the best runs. You know how that works, Ben."

"I sure do," I responded. "Anything else you might know about these men?"

"Nothing I can think of. You sound like a detective. Are you thinking of going into the railroad police force?"

"No, operating the locomotive is enough for me. I bet John Shaw, our railroad cinder dick, will be assigned the case. I think I'll give him a call." I had a natural curiosity about these things, about murders, and I think solving the George the Tyrant's murder investigation gave me some confidence that my nosiness could perhaps assist in this case.

I hung up with Ed and called John. He was an old friend and came in handy when I had questions concerning the George the Tyrant case. I dialed and John answered on the second ring as well. Two for two, I thought. "Hi, John," I said. "How's the policing coming?"

"Busy, Ben, very busy. How is it you always call when there are problems?"

"Just lucky, I guess. I'll get to the point. On the morning of the nineteenth Evans and I both saw what seemed to be a body go over the side of the haunted bridge. It was dark and foggy but we both saw the same thing, reported it to the dispatcher, and were given permission to keep moving since we hadn't hit anything. You know they found the body of James Rice in White Lick Creek. And they also found the body of Richard

Hines, crew dispatcher, under the Danville bridge. Do you know how they identified Rocko's body so rapidly?"

"Again, I don't think everyone is privy to this information, but with your nose for hunting down clues I'll answer your questions if you answer mine."

"Deal," I responded.

"To answer the James Rice question first, they found an inscription on the back of a very expensive watch, still on his person. The watch was broken and time was stopped at 6:15 AM."

"What was the inscription?" I asked.

"It was, 'Thanks, Rocko, for all the high times.' The watch was a Rolex."

"I guess that means his time of death could have been 6:15. We saw the body go over the bridge at just about that time. It sure could have been Rocko that went over the bridge."

John said, "Yes the impact from the bullet could have propelled him over the side of the bridge into the White Lick Creek."

"Have they found the cause of death of Richard Hines or time of death?"

"Still waiting on that information. Now my turn for some questions, Ben. "Do you know the conductor named Sudsy?"

"I do."

"We heard he had it in for Rocko. How is he at keeping his temper?"

"He can get hot under the collar but being bumped from a job is no reason to murder a man."

"We're going to interview him when he returns from his trip. If you think of any additional information about either of the men who lost their lives let me know, Ben."

"Okay, John. Will do." I heard the phone click from the other end.

This gave me some additional information. I added to my notes that it was very likely that the ghostly figure going over the haunted bridge was that of Rocko. He had been shot in the back. He had worn an expensive watch, a Rolex, inscribed with "Thanks, Rocko, for all the high times." The watch had stopped at 6:15 AM; the likely time of his death.

My phone rang with my work call for 1300 hours EST. That gave me some time to think on the newly discovered facts. I was also happy to know that at least part of this trip would be in the light of day.

I sat and thought about Rocko and his watch. I had noticed the watch on our last trip together. It looked expensive. Strange that a man pulled out of service for eight months would have such a timepiece. I thought about the inscription, "Thanks for all the high times." Did "high" refer to good times or drugs?

Just then my phone rang and startled me. It was Detective Robert Holman. He started by telling me that it was confirmed that the body in White Lick Creek was that of Rocko. I told him that I had just spoken with John Shaw and that he had confirmed it. He thanked me for my time and added that there was some relationship between Rocko and the crew dispatcher. That Rocko received calls from Richard Hines dispatching trains from Evansville from the Indianapolis dispatching office. He added, "We're looking further into their relationship."

I thanked him and grabbed my grip to get down to the van for my return trip home.

CHAPTER 12

SAINT LOUIS,
MARCH 24, 1300 EST

On the return trip with Lurch I recounted my conversations with Ed, John, and Detective Holman. He sat and thought for some time while intermittently calling out the signals. Then he said, "You know that the Indian worked for a while in Evansville as well. There seems to be an Evansville connection, Ben. Richard Hines, James Rice, Ed Lawson and the Indian all worked there. Or, in the case of Richard Hines, he dispatched crews there from Indianapolis. I don't know that Sudsy fits in other than he was mad at James Rice, Rocko, for bumping him off the pool. But you said the cops are interviewing him first and then interviewing Betty. I really doubt she has anything to do with this."

"I didn't know that the Indian had worked in Evansville," I said.

"I spent some long hours with him as his conductor. Engineers don't spend much time with other engineers. The Indian hated it in Evansville. He said he would always get the trips that ether didn't pay or were difficult. You know, setting at sidings and those that had the worst power as leads. The Indian had added that the same men got all the good runs. He thought he was targeted for the lousy runs because…he was Indian, Native American. So, he bumped up here."

"This is all news to me. You're right. There does seem to be an Evansville connection," I added as we neared an approach signal.

We pulled into our first siding and took out our suppers for the evening. I had a ham and cheese sandwich but added a salad from a deli without ordering a cookie and chips. Lurch took notice and asked if I were attempting another diet to reduce my big belly.

I responded, "Trying."

Lurch ate his chicken club sandwich, chips, and sipped at a diet cola.

It had been a bright sunny day. Now the sun was beginning to set behind us. I took off my sunglasses and was somewhat relieved to scan the landscape without the glare of the brilliant day. It was peaceful here, no rusty train cars to pick up, no evidence of industry, just empty fields. These fields had been plowed and the earth looked cared for, readied for spring planting, for new life.

I enjoyed moments like these on my trips. Dinner in a peaceful setting, who could ask for more.

After I finished my sandwich and salad, I could see the westbound train approaching the interlocking and, after it cleared, we were given permission to continue on our run. The rest of the trip was uneventful. My favorite kind. We arrived about 2200 hours in the Indianapolis yard. I followed Lurch into the yard office. Where he'd gone to put in our time slips. I noticed Ed sitting in a vacant office doing some paperwork.

"Working kind of late aren't you, Ed?" I commented as I stood outside the doorframe.

He looked up and replied, "Kind of busy," and looked down at his papers.

This wasn't the kindly man I had prayed with several days before. His mood was drastically different today so I moved on quickly to the locker room. I hung my jacket in the locker and left the building for home.

I entered the house. All was quiet. I didn't want to wake my wife so I just quietly slipped into my shorts and T-shirt and hit the hay. It hadn't been a bad day. I thanked God for that and fell readily into a deep sleep.

I woke the next morning to the smells of bacon and coffee. I dialed my stand number and learned I was four times out. "Yeah! "I said to myself. If Deb was free we could do something together today. I showered and followed my nose all the way to the kitchen. I hugged my wife and asked, "What do you want to do today? I have some time." Deb responded with a smile and returned hug.

She said, "That's too good to be true. Did you realize it is Palm Sunday, Ben?"

I replied happily, "I didn't realize it was Sunday, let alone Palm Sunday. So, I guess it's church, dinner out, and maybe a visit with the kid."

"You got it. It's so much more special when you're home to share the day with me."

"I do make most people's days, don't I?" I said, then smiled my winning smile as I sipped at my coffee with cream.

Deb patted me on the head and walked into the bedroom to get ready for church.

I sauntered out to the mailbox to get the Sunday paper, retrieved it, and swiped two more pieces of bacon from the plate along with my cup of coffee. I'd almost forgotten what a "normal" Sunday morning was like. It had been some time since I had had a Sunday morning at home. I hated missing church, Sunday dinners, and visits with family, but I would treasure today.

As I was reading the paper Deb returned from the bedroom looking and smelling great. I commented, "I sure did marry a good-looking woman."

She smiled. "Your turn to turn into the good-looking guy that I married, only with less hair."

"Ha," I said as I walked in the bedroom to change into church clothes.

We arrived five minutes early. Shook hands heartily, greeted others with smiles. The church itself smelled fresh of palm fronds. White Easter lilies lined the front steps of the stage, forming a floral picket fence. A cool spring breeze wafted through the side door. The children began marching down the aisles with fronds in their hands, some waving frantically, some just barely held high, and one child dragging his on the floor behind him. But the effect was not lost on the congregation as we stood and sang out, "Crown him with many crowns." The air vibrated with expectancy, with joy, with knowledge that something wonderful had happened and would happen again. Christ would return again as the King of Kings.

Palm Sunday always brought back memories of the church I attended as a kid. It was a white clapboard building situated high on a hill. Its stately bell tower could be seen for miles. The bells rang out each Sunday morning precisely five minutes before service began. We climbed the sanctuary steps with scrubbed faces and shining shoes. It was Sunday, the Lord's Day. I'm not sure my siblings and I behaved better on the Lord's Day but we attempted to do so.

I took control of my wandering mind that had drifted back in time and began to concentrate on the pastor's words. He filled us with God's Word, revived us with hope, and sustained us with God's love. He counseled us during the days our children were in the prodigal years. I appreciated our pastor. He tirelessly served the Lord.

Soon the service was over. We had decided to eat lunch at the local restaurant that was closest to our church. As we sat at our table we noticed some others from our church had the same idea. We ordered and began to chat about the week that had just passed. Deb was nearly done with another education project that involved student teachers and I caught her up with what

I knew about Rocko and Richard Hines. Then I asked her if she would be interested in taking a walk after we ate and then going to see our daughter, Liz. She said she would text Liz and see if an evening visit would work. Our meal came, pot roast, mashed potatoes, and carrots and the best buns this side of the Mississippi. While we ate, Deb got a return text that Liz was going to a friend's house to watch a basketball game in the evening. Deb responded somewhat disappointedly, "Have fun. We will make it another time."

We finished up our meal with blackberry cobbler and the dessert tipped the scale. Now we would have to walk. After arriving back at our house and changing into more appropriate walking attire we took off for the woods. I was in the driver's seat and had decided that our walk would be in the Avon park nearest the haunted bridge. I had planned a little investigating myself as we turned blackberry cobbler into pure muscle...or at least I was hoping for such an outcome.

We parked at the gazebo and began our walk. It was a nice day, in the 60s with a slight breeze. There were other adults supervising their children also trying to gain muscle or wear out their children and enjoy the day. Deb had noticed where we were and asked what we were looking for. I was glad she wasn't annoyed we came here for my investigation but was just an inquiring mind wanting to know more.

I responded, "I'm not sure, just thought we'd get as close to bridge as possible. Maybe I'd get an idea why Rocko was here in the dark."

The railroad didn't want people strolling out onto the bridge so the park path near the tracks curved in the opposite direction. Many a teen through the years found their way through the briars, thorns, and trees to the bridge. I explained this to Deb as we tried to move brush to get closer to the bridge as well. Luckily in early spring there wasn't much dense foliage.

We slowly moved thorny branches that were devoid of leaves as we walked. Once released, the thin woody stems rebounded like whips. One such stem left my hand just a little too soon, swung back and stabbed Deb on her right thigh. I apologized and slowed my pace some. We made it to the tracks and walked along them, getting closer to the bridge. She commented that she hoped we didn't meet a train on the way.

"I'm not working so they aren't running," I said and laughed at my own self-importance joke.

She didn't laugh and rubbed her thigh. I hoped a train didn't come by as well. The suction of the trains as they pass can be difficult to withstand. We saw the bridge and the walkway. I looked over the railing and saw the creek that passed underneath. It was still high from spring rains. Rocko might have survived the seventy-foot fall into high water had he not been shot. We climbed down an embankment and walked along the creek side. Deb pointed out that the briars were beginning to bud and that soon the whole area would be full of greenery and be difficult to pass through.

We continued to walk and enjoy the sound of running water and leaves crackling beneath our feet. I knew that the police had found Rocko's body on the other side of the creek, caught on a fallen tree. The other side of the creek had several fallen trees. It was the side that erosion had occurred to a greater degree as the creek changed course. We were on the park side of the creek, no fallen trees hindering our path.

We hadn't made much progress when I noticed a black handle partially obscured by leaves near the creek bank. I walked closer to the dark metal to investigate and it turned out to be just what I expected it was: a gun. I asked Deb to get out her phone and she called the Avon Police Department.

I took over the call and asked if Detective Holman was on duty. The answer was, "Who's calling?" I identified myself and stared my relationship with Detective Holman and asked again if he was on duty. The unidentified person on the other end said, "No, he's not," but added that he would give me his number since I didn't have my phone with me that contained his number. I got his number and dialed him direct. He answered and I explained to him our location as best as I could describe using the creek and what I could see on the road through the trees as landmarks. I informed him of the gun partially covered in leaves lying just beside my left foot.

He asked, "Did you touch the weapon?"

I responded that I had not. And he asked if Deb and I could wait there until he arrived.

I said, "Sure." And hung up.

We both stood there and peered down at the gun. Deb said, "Do you think this is the gun that killed Rocko?"

I was wondering that same thing as I responded, "It could be."

We seemed to be having a moment of silence for the dead conductor that no one knew very well. Deb turned and wandered about, staying within a twenty-foot radius of the gun. I don't know if she was just meditating or searching for something more. I stood guard over the ugly looking black weapon. It may have been only ten minutes, but it seemed a much longer time until we heard a siren. I started waving my arms rather frantically across the creek toward the road toward the squad car. It wasn't traveling fast and Detective Holman must have been searching for me because the car slowed and stopped. He got out and yelled that a police boat would soon be here and carry them across the swollen creek to our side. As soon as he had said the word "side" the police boat arrived.

A few minutes later Detective Holman and two other policemen were on the scene. The lights on the cars across the creek were on and cars passing by were slowing, their drivers gawking. I became more ill at ease by all of the attention. I knew Deb would be really uncomfortable. This was not turning out to be the peaceful, enjoy nature, and enjoy a rare time together day that she had hoped for. As the policemen gathered up the revolver and scanned the area for more clues, I approached my wife feeling somewhat guilty for the bad turn of events.

She asked, "Can we return to our car now?"

I turned and waved to Detective Holman indicating our departure and we began to reverse our walk and return to the car. We got back to the gazebo much more quickly than we walked away from it. There wasn't much chitchat on the return hike. I realized this was not a good sign. There wasn't much chitchat on the ride home, either. I was in trouble.

We arrived to the safety of our home. It seemed to be a welcomed port in a storm. I was surprised to see that four hours had passed since we left for our walk. I decided to sit down and watch some TV. I found a rerun of *Columbo*. My mind wasn't really concentrating on the show, but rather, on the discovery in the woods. I decided that if I were home tomorrow I would give the Danville police a call. I wanted to find out if they had found the cause of death for Richard Hines. Had he been murdered also?

Deb entered the room and asked if I would mind having frozen pizza for a quick supper. I told her that would be fine. She went to the kitchen and returned to the family room with me. She commented that seeing the gun made Rocko's death all the more real and sad, "Ben, this wasn't an ideal way to spend our day together, but I do want you to find out *who did this!*"

I guess since finding the murderer of George last fall I was now an official crime solver in her eyes. I hoped others didn't have such high expectations of me. We ate the pizza and went to bed shortly after *Columbo* had finished solving his crime. I wished that in real life there was the surety of the good guys overcoming evil as in the rerun. I put my head on the pillow and dropped into a deep sleep.

CHAPTER 13

INDIANAPOLIS,
MARCH 26, 1100 EST

The next morning, I awoke to an empty house. I spotted a short message left on the kitchen table that was void of food. The message said that my wife had left for the college and would see me when I returned from my next trip. I felt that I had really let her down on our day spent in the woods. I would have to think of a way to make it up to her. She had started the coffee and probably had her share. I poured out a big mug of the jolt juice and popped some toast in the toaster. After I slathered the toast with peanut butter I took my "single" man's breakfast into the TV room. I turned on the TV and watched the past weekend's carnage cover the screen interrupted by happy jingles selling car insurance and dish soap. I turned the television off after ten minutes. That was more than enough noise from the rectangular view into the world. I finished my toast and coffee and sat there and decided that this was good moment for prayer.

I felt uplifted after taking the violence I saw on TV and the gun discovery to the Lord. A couple of minutes had passed by and the silence in the room was broken by the ring tone. I learned I would be on the W186 at 1100 EST with Sudsy as my conductor.

I guessed that Sudsy bumped back on our board. I thought that maybe I could learn more about the investigation from Sudsy as I got up to get my shower.

After I had showered and packed my grip for the trip, I noticed that I had some time for a few calls. I was thinking of calling the Danville Police Department to learn of the cause of death of Richard Hines but realized that I really didn't have connections there. Instead, I decided to call John Shaw. I dialed his number but he didn't answer so I just left a brief message for him to give me a return call at his leisure.

I decided to give Detective Holman a call and see if he knew anything more this morning following our encounter in the woods yesterday. He answered on the fifth ring. I asked him about the gun found in the woods. He said it was a Smith and Wesson .357 magnum, model 686, six-shot gun that could deliver a great impact—strong enough to push a man from a bridge. It had only a few partial prints, none of which were of any help and the serial number that was under the cylinder under the barrel of the gun had been filed off.

The gun didn't tell the story I wanted to know so I asked if the Danville Police Department had word on the cause of death of Richard Hines. He said that the coroner's report just came in. Richard had multiple contusions and lacerations, kidney damage, a broken spine and the occipital bone was fractured. The bone fracture most probably caused his death.

"It looks as if there was a fight, he was pushed from the bridge or just lost his balance, and the bone fracture killed him. This information was forwarded to the railroad as well as our office," Detective Holman finished with a loud sigh.

I thanked him and informed him I had to be off on the next train out of town. He thanked me again for yesterday's deadly find.

I loaded my truck with my grip and decided to stop on the way to the railyard for a sandwich for lunch or supper. After I had got my meal I pulled into the yard and entered the office. I spotted Sudsy right off.

"Hey, Big Ben, looks like we have this trip together. I checked for the paperwork. It's not ready yet."

"Nothing new under heaven, Sudsy. Glad you're back on the pool. I'm going to get some coffee while we wait. Do you want a cup?" I asked.

"Nah, I have had enough for the moment. Thanks," he said as he strolled into the crew room.

I poured my coffee, rounded the corner, and saw Karen sitting at her desk. She spotted me and motioned me in.

"Hi, Karen how's the health business going?" I asked.

She responded with, "Same ole. The guys are reluctant to try and start any exercise routines until their doctors give them final warnings. When was your last walk, Ben?"

"Yesterday in the woods. Probably a two, two-and-a-half mile hike," I said with pride.

She eyed me to see if I was speaking the truth then decided I must be, and winked. She added that I was her favorite trainman.

"Thanks, Karen. Anything else new around here?"

"Can we speak in private?"

"Sure."

She stood, paused, and came around and closed the door. "Ben, I've been thinking about a conversation I overheard before Rocko was found dead. I don't know if I need to pass the information along to John Shaw or not. I don't want the guys to think I'm a gossip monger or that I can't be trusted with information. I handle primarily health information so I need to have their confidence."

"Was the conversation concerning health?" I asked.

"No, it wasn't."

"Do you think it would help in the investigation of Rocko's murder?"

"It may, I'm not sure."

"Do you want to tell me?"

"I do. I need to tell someone. I can't keep it to myself any longer. It's keeping me awake. And I know I can trust you."

"Okay, let's hear."

Karen told me that Ed Lawson and the Indian were arguing outside her office. She added that overhearing management and trainmen arguing was nothing new but that she heard conversations mentioning Rocko. The Indian said that Rocko had no business working on the railroad at all let alone here in Indianapolis. He told Ed that he knew that this was true and that Ed could do something about it and should do something about it. He had the authority and responsibility to do something about it. Finally, the Indian stomped off and threatened to take matters into his own hands if Ed didn't or wouldn't.

Upon finishing Karen asked, "I just don't know, Ben. Do I need to take this information to John Shaw, the investigator, or not? I don't want to plant suspicion. I've been wrestling with repeating this conversation to John. I'm also wrestling with wondering if I, too, have a mistrust of police, white policemen in particular. I thought that I'd escaped many prejudices common to my race. But I seem to have a distrust of white policeman. I'm still exploring that in myself."

"Karen, you keep exploring. You're one of the finest young women I know. We all need to explore prejudices and work to keep God's love, justice, and truth in our lives. You are my sister in Christ. I know you will decide on the right thing." I stood and added, "I'll keep you in my prayers today. God will speak wisdom to you. I know you wanted a 'yes, go forward with the information' or a 'no.' My daughters get angry with me for advising them to search themselves and ask God for wisdom, but you're exploring your soul and I know that's a good thing." I left her with that and ran into Sudsy just outside her office door.

He said, "Got the paperwork and ready to go."

I threw my coffee cup into the trash and walked to the van waiting to take us to our train.

The driver was Chuck. I greeted him and asked about his wife.

"She's doing much better. The last round of chemo seems to have her in remission. She's still embarrassed by the lack of hair but will come out with me on occasion with the new wig I bought her. Thanks for asking."

"I'm glad to hear this," I responded.

We continued talking until we arrived at the train, ready to relieve the tired crew that had worked all night and half the day. We boarded and got permission to be on our way.

Sudsy started the conversation I was interested in. "I'm glad to be back on this pool. But you need to know that I would not kill a man to get the position back. I think some of the guys think I would. They walk to the other side of a hallway and look down, never making eye contact."

I wasn't making eye contact either but was watching the screens on the locomotive as Sudsy continued on.

"You know, Ben, John Shaw called me in the office and questioned me on my relationship with Rocko. He asked all kinds of questions like 'How long have I known him?' 'What was my last conversation with him?' 'Did I threaten him?' 'What was the day and time I last saw him?' 'What was I doing on March nineteenth around

6:00 AM?' John asked the same questions slightly different over and over again. I don't like being thought of as a possible murderer. I would not kill a man for a position on a pool no matter how much I needed the money."

"I guess John is just doing his job, Sudsy. He needs to find out who did this terrible thing. Say, why were you so angry about being bumped from the pool, anyway? You know it's just union rules in action."

"I just bought a new truck, have a house payment, and owe child support. I can't make it on the extra-board pay. I finally had enough seniority to keep my position on the Saint Louis pool, or so I thought. Then this Rocko comes from out of nowhere and bumps me. He wasn't nice to the guys either, Ben. Maybe he made a real enemy. I was mad. But not murder mad!"

Sudsy called out "approach" as we moved closer to the next signal. I slowed the train. The dispatcher radioed that we would need to pull into the next siding. I responded in the affirmative and maneuvered the train off the main track.

I looked over at Sudsy who was reading a mechanics magazine while appearing rather morose. He was in his early forties and had close cropped mousy colored hair. The kind that matches his skin color. His eyes were set just a little too close together and his lips rather thin. He had a thick neck and sturdy build, but at the moment he looked like a large child saddened by some tragic bit of news. Since he quieted I sat and thought about this man with whom I had worked for some years now. He was like many a trainman who thought their fortunes were finally assured in this business when they could hold a pool job, trains were moving, and business was good. They accelerated their spending not realizing business fluctuates and slows, men get moved from pool to pool, and some get put back on the extra-board. The extra–board contains men or woman who substitute for any missed calls by trainmen on the assigned pools. The extra-board results in generally much smaller paychecks that vary greatly from pay period to pay period. When I first started working at an engineer's rate of pay my paychecks could vary as much as $2,000 dollars from one to the next. It was a very precarious lifestyle. I was cautious. I didn't know if the next check would cover the water bill, let alone my mortgage. Some of the guys get careless and overspend as soon as two checks in a row are good ones. Sudsy had made the same mistake as countless other trainmen. I thought, would the man sitting so near to me take a life for a pool position?

The train dispatcher radioed that we would be here for a while so I took out my phone and opened it to my notes concerning Rocko. I could fill in some more facts and questions.

NOTES

I just reiterated the fact, number 1, The body found in White Lick Creek was that of Rocko, James Rice.

I typed the answer "yes" to question 2, which was Saw figure go over side of haunted bridge on March 19th approximately 0600 EST. Was the figure that of Rocko? Yes.

For question number 3, Cause of death was gunshot wound in back. Need to find out how they identified the body so quickly. I typed Found watch on body. It was engraved with "Thanks, Rocko, for the high times."

Didn't know the answer to question 4, Why was Rocko out on the train bridge the day after we discussed it in the van?

The answer to question 5 was that Rocko missed the call because he was lying in White Lick Creek, dead.

For question number 6, Body found under bridge in Danville. It was that of dispatcher Richard Hines. Need to find out time and cause of death. Why was crew dispatcher out on train bridge or under it in early morning? I knew part of answer and typed March 19th between 7:00 and 11:00 AM.

For question 7, What was the cause of death of crew dispatcher? I typed in lacerations, contusions, fracture of spine and occipital bone. He either fell or was pushed from bridge.

The answer to question 8, Did Rocko and crew dispatcher know one another? was "yes. Rocko was crew dispatched by Richard Hines in Evansville."

My notes now looked like I had made some progress.

Most of my original questions now had answers. But, I had more questions to add.

ADDITIONAL QUESTIONS

1. What was the conversation between Ed and the Indian really about and how is it related to these deaths? If at all?
2. Is there an Evansville connection?
3. How does Sudsy fit in?
4. How does Betty fit in?

After I typed in my last questions I thought I would type out my suspect and possible motive list.

SUSPECT AND MOTIVES

-   Sudsy, motive - needed position on pool to make money to cover his current expenses.
-   Betty,-motive - unknown
-   Indian - thinks Rocko should not be working on railroad?
-   Ed - Knows more about Rocko and accused by the Indian of allowing Rocko to work on railroad when he should not be?
-   Richard Hines - Why is he in the mix of all this? What is the relationship between Richard and Rocko?

I had just finished my notes when the train dispatcher gave us the signal to head west. I turned off my phone and placed it back into my grip. Sudsy put his magazine down and we proceeded toward Saint Louis.

Sudsy dropped the conversation concerning Rocko's death and he asked if I knew anything about the death of Richard Hines the crew dispatcher. I told him what I had learned that morning and he just replied with a drawn out "Hmmm."

As we approached the next siding, Sudsy called out in his squeaky voice, "Approach."

I knew we would not be getting off duty anytime soon so we entered the siding and decided it was time for supper and ate and talked of the latest safety rules adopted by our employer. The last of our trip was in the dark. We were given permission to enter the Saint Louis yard and to go off duty at 2230 hours. We made it in before we were outlawed. But it still had been a long day.

I didn't know our limo driver. He was new and middle-aged. That was unusual in itself. Usually the drivers were working after they retired from another job or the drivers were young, just beginning a career. Middle age was an anomaly. The man's name was Dave. He said that he had lost his job as a restaurant manager. But, he was glad to be out of that field and looking forward to just driving. He seemed pleasant enough as he hailed us good night.

Sudsy and I entered the hotel and got our room assignments and cookies to go. I asked Sudsy if he wanted to eat breakfast tomorrow. He replied he did. I walked down the hall, unlocked the door, and pulled it closed behind me.

CHAPTER 14

SAINT LOUIS,
MARCH 27, 1600 EST

slept very well. It seemed like five minutes had passed since I laid my head on the pillow the night before. I got up and opened the curtains to be greeted by a dreary drizzle. I made some coffee in the room and ate my cookie from last night's check in. After I finished getting dressed in my jeans, T-shirt and flannel shirt, my phone rang. I picked it up and Sudsy asked if I was ready for breakfast. I replied that I would meet him in the hotel restaurant in five minutes and hung up to pack my grip for the return train trip home. I met Sudsy at the table nearest the kitchen door. The kitchen noise reminded me of home. The smells of coffee, toast, and eggs frying always elevated my mood. I never minded being located near the kitchen in a restaurant.

"How was your night?" he asked.

"Perfect," I said. "Slept like a baby."

"I wish I could have. Not sleeping well these days. You might have to keep me awake on the return trip."

"I'll give you an elbow if I hear you snoring. I need to hear the signals called out tonight so I'll stay awake as well."

The waitress came by and took our breakfast orders while she poured our coffee. I sipped at my coffee and told Sudsy that if he would drink more coffee than usual then he would surely stay awake for the trip home.

Sudsy sipped at his and asked, "Ben, did you like Rocko?"

I thought for a moment before I replied, curious as to why Sudsy was asking my opinion of a man so recently murdered. "I only worked with him one time and he had seemed very reluctant to talk, I wasn't sure if it was because the other guys were giving him a hard time or that was just his nature. I'm not sure how I felt about the man. He was quiet, maybe too quiet. However, I'm sure he didn't deserve to be shot in the back."

"I didn't like him. But you're right. No man deserves that," Sudsy replied in an octave somewhat higher than usual.

We both began to eat our breakfasts. When I finished, I told Sudsy I was going back to my room to wait for the work call. He sat at the table stacked with dirty plates and looked down at his phone as it rang. I turned and walked away.

I returned to my room and sat on the over-stuffed chair. I was trying to decide whether to turn on the TV when my phone rang. Ed Lawson. I answered, "Hi, Ed, how's it going?"

"Not well, Ben. I was called into John Shaw's office. He asked me all kinds of questions concerning Rocko. I think that since I knew him in Evansville I've become a suspect in his murder. I can't believe it. It's bad enough that the powers that be are always on my case to pull more trainmen out of service, but I'm now a suspect in a murder investigation. I heard you're somewhat of a crime solver, Ben. You better solve this one and quickly."

The word "quickly" was followed by a sound that clearly indicated our conversation was at an end.

Before I had a moment to think my phone rang again. It was Betty. "Hi, Betty," I answered.

"Ben, I need your help."

"What can I do for you?" I responded. She went on to tell me of her conversation with John Shaw as well. She had been questioned and also felt that she was now a suspect. Betty used some colorful words interspaced with cursing to describe John. She added, "Who would think a seventy-plus year-old-woman would be walking around a haunted bridge in the dark of early morning with a gun?"

My guess was that she used those same colorful words with John. I calmed her down and told her that John was just doing his job. Then I asked her, "What made you ask about the bridge on the trip home that last time you chauffeured Rocko and me?"

That riled her up all over again. Betty's gravelly voice rang out over the phone for the next five minutes straight. The gist of the matter seemed to be that she overheard the Indian and the Mad Russian talking about it two days before that trip. She was just curious about the facts concerning the bridge, if there were any. And she added, "Can't an old woman just be curious?" Betty was demonstrating how upset she really was by referring to herself as an "old woman." She wasn't one to admit to age. She hung up rather abruptly, as well.

This wasn't my day. Then the phone rang again with the news that I was to be on the E173 at 1600 EST.

I decided I needed a good rerun on television to relax with while waiting for my van ride to the railyard. I switched on the TV and found *Wagon Train*. Maybe this would clear my mind, I thought as I closed the drapes to reduce the glare on the television. While watching the show the jostling of the wagon train reminded me of the slack action on the locomotive. But I had to admit I'd rather be on the worst of coal trains than a wagon train of yesteryear. I decided to be grateful for train slack action. As the show was coming to a happy conclusion my phone rang yet again. I answered with, "Ben Time here."

Detective Holman said, "Hi, Ben, I just wanted to let you know that the bullet found in Rocko was matched to the Smith and Wesson you discovered in the woods. So, you did find the murder weapon."

"Oh." I was temporarily out of words. Detective Holman said they were sending more policemen back out there to the haunted bridge vicinity to do a more thorough search. I said my good bye and after hanging up I had decided to write some more information in my notes.

Betty didn't seem to have a connection with Rocko. She was just curious about the haunted bridge. I also added that the weapon used to murder Rocko was a Smith and Wesson .357 magnum. My gut feeling was that I could cross Sudsy off the suspect list but still didn't have evidence to do so. Ed had been acting strangely during our last two conversations. The Indian had been brought up several times in this investigation and I knew almost nothing about the crew dispatcher, Richard Hines. I thought I might start looking into him further. I knew a retired dispatcher who had also worked out of Indianapolis. His name was Dave Colbert. He was dispatching crews for the Chicago area and the runs westward out of Indianapolis. When he was a working dispatcher he was polite, and treated us trainmen like people not machines. I had liked Dave. I thought I might give him a call when *Wagon Train* was over and see what he knew about the mysterious Richard Hines.

I didn't get to call Dave Colbert because I had nodded off again, but instead gathered up the contents of my grip and left the room. When I reached the automatic glass doors the van was waiting with Sudsy already seated in the front. I threw my grip in the back of the van and followed. Sudsy greeted me with, "It's about time you got here."

I responded with, "I'm not late." Then I asked the driver to stop by the sandwich place for the usual. Sudsy said he wanted a sandwich to go as well. We chose our subs, chips, and soda. "No cookies for me," I told Sudsy. "I have to watch my figure."

He said, "You should have started years ago, Ben."

"Better late than never," I responded. I held the door for the next customer entering, as we were exiting.

Our paperwork was ready and we were chauffeured to the train. The crew got off wordlessly and we got on. The smell of diesel fuel lingered in the air. We made our preparations to leave, were given permission by the yardmaster and train dispatcher to move forward, and off we went toward home. Sudsy called the signals and we had little conversation as I brought the train up to speed.

I decided to ask Sudsy what he knew of the crew dispatcher, Richard Hines. He said he didn't know anything about the man. He didn't think Hines had ever dispatched any of the trains he had been on. Then Sudsy asked if I had thought the two deaths were related. I told him that I thought they probably were. How often were two men found on the same day, dead under railroad bridges? It had to be more than coincidence.

The majority of this trip was in the dark and was a quiet one. We returned to Indianapolis yard and were not delayed entering so we found ourselves off duty in eight hours and thirty minutes. A good run.

I returned to my favorite girl who was sawing logs as I slid under the covers in the dark of night.

CHAPTER 15

INDIANAPOLIS, MARCH 28, 0900 EST

awoke at 0900. A good time to wake for the day. I much preferred normal hours, morning wake times, rather than waking for the day in the evening or in the middle of the night. Being forced to change from a morning person to a vampire every other day or so was very hard on my body. I lost track of time, date, and day of the week. I was often unsure when it was really time for a meal. I got headaches, felt exhausted most of the time, and the doctor gave me multiple warnings about this lack-of-scheduled lifestyle. However, this was my job, it paid the bills. And I counted down the months until retirement.

I walked into the kitchen and saw the note on the table. Which meant I missed my wife again. The note indicated that she missed me but had to be at the college early. She left some scrambled eggs and bacon in the microwave. I hoped I would still be home when she returned at the end of her day. There were some months we communicated solely through notes due to mismatched schedules.

I poured some leftover coffee, warmed my plate for one minute, and took both coffee and nourishment into the family room. *Perry Mason* was on and I noticed that he had Paul Drake to search out the details. I decided that I needed a Paul Drake as well to help with my current dilemma. Then immediately thought of Lurch. I would give him a call later. When *Perry Mason* ended I thought I would give Dave Colbert a call to learn more about Richard Hines. I could do some fact finding.

I grabbed my phone. Then I searched for Dave's phone number. I touched the screen appropriately and Dave answered on the third ring. Since I hadn't talked to Dave in about three years, I decided to reintroduce myself. He remembered me and said that he was definitely enjoying retirement. I explained the discovery of the two bodies under the bridges or close to the bridges. He didn't know Rocko but did know Richard Hines. He was sorry to hear of his passing. This comment was said in the general sort of way we all respond upon hearing of someone's demise. I asked him what he knew about the man's character. He was silent for some time. I almost thought the call was dropped but then he said that their supervisors had looked into the trains that Richard dispatched more than once. There seemed to be a lot of complaints about order of trains dispatched and to whom.

"At first I thought it was just the usual complaints of jealous trainmen too concerned about who got the deadheads home or who got an easy run. But there seemed to be more to the complaints. The supervisors threatened Richard's job more than once. Richard wasn't a nice man. I hate to speak ill of the dead, Ben."

"Do you think someone may have wanted him dead?" I asked.

"That's a pretty difficult question. I don't know the details of his life. But, he did make a lot of enemies with trainmen and with coworkers. He was the type of man found in many a novel that bites the dust for good reason. So, I'm not altogether surprised at this news. I am, however, surprised that he was found bruised and broken under a train bridge. Is this just general curiosity about the man?"

"It is in a way but I had just worked with Rocko the day before his death and to find a crew dispatcher dead under a bridge the same day is really more than coincidence. I had some success in crime solving a year ago and I guess I'm hooked."

We talked about retirement from that point on. I hung up with envy in my heart for Dave's new life, void of dispatching crews.

I checked my stand number on the automated system. I was two times out, second in line for a train. I pushed several more choices on the automated menu and learned that Lurch was at home and was three times out. I would give him some more time to rest in case he was sleeping, then interrupt him with a call. As I was reclining in my favorite chair I remembered that I had purchased oil for my truck several months back. Today would be a good day to get it changed.

I replaced my old clothes with even older clothes. These had holes in the armpits, stains from several previous oil changes and several paint jobs. My wife had tried to dispose of them at least three times. I kept pulling them from the trash, rescue 911. I needed these clothes for just such jobs as today's. In fact, I hid these deep in the depths of the closet to keep them from my wife's attempt to dispose of them again. I have discovered throughout my life that if I needed to hide something it was best concealed among like things: Clothes among clothes; fishing lures among lures; and tools among tools. I rationalized the act of hiding things to save my wife from unnecessary worry and stress...and words.

It was well after lunch when I finished changing the oil. The job went rather smoothly and I was feeling accomplished. I fixed a peanut butter and strawberry jam sandwich with a side of chips. I poured a large glass of milk and got it all to the table without dropping or spilling, another accomplishment to be proud of. I thought that this was turning out to be a wonderful day. After finishing my delightful lunch I decided to give Lurch a call. Lurch answered on the third ring.

"Hey, Ben. How's it going?"

"Good. I was afraid I would interrupt your beauty sleep...for more than one reason." I chuckled. Lurch didn't.

"Did you hear that Ed Lawson pulled the Indian and the Mad Russian out of service?"

"No! What was the violation?" I asked feeling somewhat betrayed by the man I prayed with.

"I think it was a speed violation within the yard. I'm not sure of miles per hour over. The guys said they weren't violating. The whole episode was causing quite an uproar. Maybe Ed's changing over to the dark side. Most of the guys like him but I'm not sure that will stay that way. I suppose when the speed tapes are examined it will clear everything up but it won't make Ed very popular one way or another."

I told Lurch that I was surprised at this turn of events for the most part because it involved Ed who was reluctant to turn guys in, and the Indian who, according to Karen, had threatened Ed. In fact, I was so surprised I had forgotten why I called Lurch to begin with. I hung up and decided it was time for a power nap since I would probably be working all night.

***

The phone rang and I picked it up trying to clear the fog from my brain. The automated voice informed me I would be on the W645 at 1900 with Lurch. I was glad once again that Lurch would be my conductor. I stood and walked somewhat unsteadily to the kitchen. Surprised to see my wife cooking dinner and enjoying the aroma of potatoes and onions frying in the pan, I greeted her with a smooch.

"Glad to see you for the moment. I just got my work call and need to be on my way by 1830," I said.

She responded with, "I thought the phone rang and it was your work call. At least we can have dinner together. It'll be ready by the time you're showered and ready."

I turned and walked back the direction from which I came. I never wanted to be called late for dinner.

The kitchen table was set when I returned and the food plated. Fried potatoes and onions, pork chops, applesauce and green beans. I asked if the applesauce was homemade and much to my surprise and delight it was. Deb talked some about a few of her favorite students and some about her least favorite. I talked about the most recent facts concerning the deaths of the two railroad employees. We cleared the table together and loaded the dishwasher.

"Oh, by the way," I said, "I got the oil changed in the truck. Do you want me to stop and get oil for the car?" I asked.

"No, I can get it changed for about the same price and it's not due for a change yet. Do you want me to pack a lunch for your trip? We have leftovers of our supper you can take."

"Yes, that would be wonderful," I said as I walked back toward the bedroom to pack my grip.

Deb was in the family room watching the news when I returned packed and ready to leave. She gave me a kiss and told me to take care and tell Lurch "Hi" from her. I grabbed my lunch off the kitchen counter, boarded my truck, and was off to work.

It was dark by the time I reached the Indianapolis railyard. I had just opened the door to the yard office when Indiana's loud voice greeted me. It was like meeting a miniature tornado when meeting up with Indiana. He proceeded to tell me all his most recent complaints and ended with a warning to watch out for Ed Lawson. Ed was now taking prisoners.

Then Indiana stomped out into the brisk night air. I saw Lurch in the locker room. He informed me that our paperwork was ready and we could board the train. I picked my work jacket from my locker and out we went. I was surprised that both paperwork and train were ready to leave. I stood outside the locomotive for a few minutes. I liked feeling the rumble of the earth beneath my feet just before the big step up into the vibrating machine. We had three locomotives tonight, sufficient power for the well over a mile of cars lagging behind. I groaned as I lifted myself and my grip up that first step. Lurch's grip was already in the cab. He was walking the train as I started my preparations to leave. We each preformed our jobs with the minimal of communication necessary. I liked working with Lurch because he was a good conductor. He did his work well and took pride in doing it well, and he stayed awake for the trip.

We were given permission to exit the yard. The locomotives began doing their work and we were soon on our way. We almost immediately arrived at the haunted bridge. I noticed that both of us were peering into the black of night.

Lurch said, "I wonder if the haunted bridge stories from long ago have any truth in them? I looked them up on the web the other night. I also found some ghost stories about the Danville bridge as well. Do you think it is just coincidental that two men's lives were taken in the area of these haunted bridges?"

"I don't think the deaths of Rocko and Richard Hines are due to ghosts. Ghosts don't carry guns and/or beat people up and push them from bridges. However, I do think that their deaths are related. When we get to the Effingham siding we need to review the facts of the case. I think that's why I called you today, to review the facts, and then I forgot when you informed me of Ed Lawson pulling the Indian and the Mad Russian out of service. I'll explain later."

Lurch called the next signal and on we traveled, both deep in our own thoughts.

CHAPTER 16

EFFINGHAM SIDING, MARCH 29, 0100 EST

We pulled into the siding. It was one in which there was very little light, a diffuse light from a single industry several miles away. It was a lonely place, one into which I pulled a train many a time with a sleeping conductor. At this siding, I felt I was the lone spectator of a great sleeping world.

I pulled out my phone and opened my notes app. I read them over to myself first then read them aloud to Lurch, one of a few conductors who would not be sleeping. He listened with those big ears of his. We were both silent for a moment.

Then Lurch asked, "Why do you think Richard Hines dispatched certain trains to his favorites? Was one of his favorites Rocko? Do we know where these trains went and what were they carrying?"

"Good questions, Lurch. I'll try and find out from Dave Colbert. Do you remember him? He used to dispatch crews on the west end before he retired. He's the one who gave me the few notes on Richard that I do have. He has a great memory."

"I remember him. He was all right. How's he enjoying retirement?"

"Good, I'll call him again. Maybe have lunch with him."

"Well, back to the case, Sherlock. Let's assume Rocko was one of Richard's favorites. The Indian complained about the dispatching irregularities and thought Rocko got all the good runs. Who would hate both Rocko and Richard enough to kill them?"

"Another good question, but we have too many assumptions, Watson. One, that Rocko was a favorite of Richard and two, that both men were hated and killed by same person."

Lurch got quiet again then shook his head and said he thought they were both valid assumptions, but that he would think on them some more.

The radio came alive and we were given permission to move out of the siding and be on our way.

Lurch called the signals and I thought more about the relationship between the Indian and Ed.

I liked both men. Ed did seem to be acting a bit strange lately, unlike the man I prayed with a week back. The Indian was a "normal" trainman. He had good days and bad days like most of us. He could be cantankerous from lack of sleep, frustration, etc. We all had those days.

For the most part, he played the rail game by abiding by the rules. I think he told me he was a Miami Native American, a tribe local to Indiana. He would occasionally threaten to take a scalp of one of the other trainmen, Indiana in particular, but he was just playing a part. I liked the Indian as well.

I would need to talk to both the Indian and Ed to find out more about their current feud.

Lurch and I were both getting tired as the trip wore on. It seemed that most of the night trips I would get my sleepiest about 0600. If I could just make it until the sun rose I would be all right till the end of the run. I started to sing a country western song to keep awake. Lurch looked over and gave me the stink eye then began to hum along. We both needed to stay awake and harmonized quite nicely. After a rousing rendition of "Do You Think My Tractor's Sexy?" a dispatcher came on the radio and gave us permission to enter the yard. I brought the ponies in and we dismounted our train in the light of day.

Betty picked us up in the van. She looked her age. I asked her how she was doing. She said fine but would be better when they found Rocko's murderer.

She added, "I won't really feel that I'm not a suspect until they do, Ben." Then she paused and asked if I had ideas who the murderer might be.

"I don't yet have the answers. But Lurch and I are working on it. If you hear any facts that might be pertinent, give Lurch or me a call," I said as I exited the van.

Both Lurch and I checked in, got our cookies, and made it to our respective rooms. By the time I unloaded my grip I was ready to hit the hay. I awoke at 2100. I laid there for a while after I checked my watch. I wasn't energized enough to move. I knew it would once again be dark outside which further decreased my motivation to move. It was amazing how much more motivated to wake and move I was in the daylight. I think I laid there a full half hour then decided if I wanted to eat I better get up and shower. The shower brought me to full alert status. I descended in the elevator and asked Steve, the front desk man, if he had seen Lurch. He said he had seen him just a few minutes before and he left a message for me. I asked what that message might be.

Steve responded, "Meet him at Donaly's, Restaurant."

"Thanks, Steve," I said as I walked out the automatic doors. Donaly's was just across the parking lot from the hotel so it only took a minute to get there and get seated.

Lurch looked up from studying his menu and greeted me. "Hi Ben."

"Did you rest well?" I asked.

"Slept like a baby. It must be due to my clean living."

"Your clean living and good looks," I replied and chuckled.

The waitress came to the table and we both ordered our breakfasts and coffees. Breakfast settled well on the stomach no matter the time of day.

"I think we'll get called to return home in an hour or so," I said as I closed the menu in front of me.

Lurch agreed with my assessment of our future travel plans. "Yeah, I checked the stand number before I came over."

"I guess my phone calls to Dave Colbert and to the Indian will have to wait until tomorrow.

"Have you thought of any additional questions, assumptions or facts?"

"I still think there's an Evansville link that we are missing. We need to know more about what was going on there with both Richard Hines and Rocko."

"You could be right." I sipped at my coffee.

The breakfasts were suddenly placed in front of us like manna from heaven. The waitress asked if it looked all right as we began shoveling the food in. We both shook our heads like two baseball bobbleheads and continue to shovel. Just upon finishing up, my phone rang with the "Don't Worry Be Happy" ring tone. The dispatcher informed me that I would be on a train in two hours heading home, the E478. I informed the crew dispatcher that I would tell Lurch and that he was sitting right next to me.

We finished our breakfasts and walked back across the parking lot to get ready for our return trip.

I went upstairs to repack my grip. I had a little time before I had to be downstairs waiting for the van so I decided to write down some additional questions for Dave.

QUESTIONS

Do you know what run or runs were considered the favorites that Richard was dispatching? Where was/were the train or trains headed? What was their cargo?

I then wrote some questions down for the Indian.

Same as above for Dave, plus what was going on between him and Ed?

I put my phone away and descended for the return trip home.

CHAPTER 17

SAINT LOUIS,
MARCH 30, 0100 EST

The limo driver was once again an unfamiliar face. The limo company must have been on a hiring spree. Both Lurch and I introduced ourselves. He seemed rather surprised at our introductions. He introduced himself as Roscoe, van driver and guitar player extraordinaire. I liked this guy. He had a good sense of humor. By the time we reached the yard I was fully awake and ready for the trip home. Lurch went about his paperwork thing and I got one more cup of coffee for the road, thinking I might need it to enjoy the hotel cookies stored in my grip as emergency rations.

This train was waiting and ready in the yard. We both began our preparations to leave. Ten minutes later we were given permission to be on our way home. The lights in the yard dimmed behind us as we progressed into the blackness of rural Illinois.

This trip passed by uneventfully. Even the time passed by quickly as we talked about car mechanics, changing oil, and the new computer systems that now have infiltrated the automotive and railroad industries. We arrived in Indianapolis about 0800 EST. It was a very bright spring morning. When we disembarked the temperature was in the high fifties. It was going to be a beautiful day.

I entered the yard office and passed by John's office door. His head was down and he seemed to be studying some paperwork on his desk. I thought I would put some extra clothing in my locker and stop back by his office. After I placed my jacket in the locker and shut the door, I turned to see Ed Lawson blocking the entrance.

"Hi, Ed," I said noticing that his eyes were bloodshot and his hair rumpled.

"I saw you just got off your train and thought we could have a talk."

"Sure," I replied and sat down on the narrow bench.

"Do you have any ideas who may have murdered Rocko?"

"No, but I have been thinking about it. I have a few questions for you that may help me come to some conclusions in this case."

"Shoot, Ben. I think John feels that I had something to do with this. He needs to focus on the Indian."

"Why did the Indian think that Rocko should be out of service completely, fired, and that you could do or should have done something about it?"

"How did you know that?" Ed asked in his most threatening tone.

His tone initially angered me but I held my anger in check and replied, "The conversation was held here in the yard office. Any number of trainmen could have over heard," I said, not wanting to reveal Karen as my source.

"I didn't pull the Indian out of service because of that conversation. If you know about our conversation, others do too. You'll see when they get the speed tapes off the engine. The Indian was speeding."

"I didn't ask that question. I asked why the Indian thought Rocko should have been fired. And thought you could have done something about it."

"I told you before that Rocko had trouble with drugs. He went to rehab and finished his treatment and bumped up here. The Indian must have thought that I should have pulled him out of service again." Ed raised his voice an octave as he turned to walk out. "I don't know why." He let the door slam behind him.

I sat there a moment wondering at the change in character I had seen in this man in the last week or so. I gathered up my grip and started toward John's door. I knocked and he looked up.

"Hi, Ben. How's the train business going?"

"Last run was great. I wish they were all like that. Hey, John, I have some information on the Rocko–Richard Hines case. I would like to trade information and see what you know. Sound good?"

"Only with you, Ben. I know you're trustworthy and can be an aid in murder cases. It seems that Detective

Holman trusts you as well. But don't, for a minute, think I do this with just anyone."

"I know, John, and I appreciate your trust. What do you know about Richard Hines? In particular, there seemed to be some complaints about how he dispatched trains in Evansville."

"Boy, Ben, you sure do hear the rumors, rumors that may be pertinent to the case."

"I do," I said as I took out my phone with my notes. I read the questions and answers that I had listed under my notes app and slowed when I got to my questions concerning the train runs in Evansville that other conductors complained about.

John furiously wrote as I spoke, then he turned to his notes and answered the train run questions that he had previously looked up. "The two runs that had the most complaints were the N893 and S461. The N893 went north to a warehouse and dropped two cars off close to Roselake. The S461 returned from Roselake, picked up two cars at the same warehouse and returned to Evansville. The runs were fast ones so most conductors and engineers liked them, off duty early." John shifted his position, glanced back down at his notes and continued, "The funny thing, Ben, was that the engineer roster was dispatched correctly but the conductor roster was definitely not. Rocko got most of those runs. There was definitely something shady about that. When Rocko was in rehab the runs were dispatched correctly. We think that's when Richard Hines' supervisor threatened him that if crews weren't correctly dispatched he would lose his job.

For the next six months crews were dispatched without irregularities. But we have noticed that Richard Hines recently bumped to dispatch crews to the Indianapolis westbound board at the same time that Rocko bumped here."

Too many coincidences. I finished writing down these notes and agreed with John. I kept wondering why Richard Hines bumped to the Indianapolis west board.

John added, "Ben, this has to remain between you and me. I know I can trust you and that you too are seeking the truth."

"I'll keep it to myself, John. One more question. Are you suspicious of Ed Lawson?"

"I don't want to be, but something isn't kosher between him and the Indian. I agree there is definitely an Evansville connection. Keep me in the loop. Your notes have been a big help."

I ended the conversation with agreeing to keep John in the loop and left the yard office for home.

CHAPTER 18

INDIANAPOLIS, MARCH 31, 0930 EST

I arrived home about 9:30 in the morning. Deb was not home. I still had a modicum of energy and went out to the perennial garden. I had trimmed back most plant life last fall. Looking down at the dark brown earth and the fragments of black mulch I noticed some signs of life. The green stems of the daffodils were standing upright defying the cold and frost and the tulips were just beginning to push through the bleak landscape. I thought that I would most probably have to re-mulch the garden next month. I would ask Deb to be on the lookout for a good sale on the black wood chip.

I sat down on the garden glider and thanked the Lord for His goodness and the new life rising from the earth. God leaves hints of His plan, that of eternal life, all over creation. I thanked Him for His promise of eternal life, for His good plan.

My mind wandered and I started to think about Ed Lawson. Could the man I prayed with about pulling men out of service unnecessarily be guilty of murder? He had behaved strangely lately, more abrupt with his questions and answers, more secretive, angrier, or perhaps fearful. I know that even the followers of our Lord fall but could Ed have fallen so far as to murder a fellow trainman? I thought that I really needed to talk with him away from the railroad, away from interruptions.

I was getting tired and ready to hit the hay. I walked into the house and fell into a good sleep.

It seemed like only minutes had passed when I awoke to the smell of Deb's meatloaf and fresh rolls baking. I loved that smell. It meant home, Deb, and dinner! I got up, showered, and dressed. When I arrived in the kitchen the table was set and the food was being placed in the center of the old oak slab. Deb looked up at me as she finished setting the mashed potatoes down. "I knew the smell would bring you to life. It always does!"

"It's amazing how that works," I said. "How was your day?" I asked as I pulled out her chair for her.

"Fine. I handed in the last of the student teachers' reports. This was a good group. They'll make great teachers. How was your trip?"

"Uneventful. The kind I like. I found out a few more facts about the Rocko case. But the more I find out the more questions I add to my notes. The dispatcher who died had some nefarious connection with Rocko. I'm thinking Rocko may have been working for Richard Hines and setting out some train cars, either delivering something illegal or picking something up illegal, because a conductor would be the one to see that certain cars are set out. The engineer has nothing to do with setting cars out at an industry. The conductor actually runs that show. When the trains were dispatched, only the conductors' board was mishandled and Rocko got the same run. Richard Hines bumped from dispatching one board to another to follow Rocko. You know, Deb, I just put this all together now. Sleep does a body good!"

"Good job, Ben! But who killed Rocko?"

"I don't know that yet. I need to check up on a few more facts." I took another bite of meatloaf. "I may make a call after dinner, or do you have some plans?"

"I don't have any plans. Maybe just some TV."

We ate the rest of dinner talking about our daughters and trying to come up with a time for a visit to Oklahoma to visit Trish. After agreeing that the first week in the month of June would work for us and finishing up our dinner dishes Deb decided she would call Trish to see if that week would work for her and I would call Ed Lawson to feel him out about what was going on in his life. Deb went upstairs to her office for her call and I went into the TV room for mine.

Ed's son answered the phone and called for his dad. The boy didn't yell into the phone and was extremely polite. Ed and his wife were teaching him well. Ed answered with, "Hello, Ed Lawson here."

I responded in kind. "Hi, Ed, this is Ben Time. I just wanted to touch base with you and see how you are doing? We didn't end our last conversation on a good note and I think too much of you to let a misunderstanding cloud our relationship. Is everything okay?"

Ed kind of stuttered and stammered and indicated that everything was fine then got quiet. After a short pause, he said, "No, everything is not fine. Ben, I know you prayed for me. I pulled the Indian out of service because he was exceeding the speed limit through the yard. It was a very real violation. The speed tape didn't get pulled and the engine moved on. They still haven't caught up with the engine and pulled the tapes. The Indian will not be pulled out of service if the tapes are not returned to this yard office in two days. I now look just like most management employees, out to get the guys, and that's what I am not. I have worked very hard to gain the trainmen's trust. On top of this John thinks I may have something to do with Rocko's death. That's the most disturbing thing on my current list of disturbing things. I have nothing to do with the murder and in our last conversation you seemed to agree with John."

"I just wanted to know why the Indian accused you of allowing Rocko to work when, according to the Indian, he shouldn't have been working. What's the story behind the accusation?"

"When I was an engineer about twenty years ago, a road foreman pulled me out of service. He hid in the bushes like a weed weasel and set me up for a failure. I had no out-of-service insurance, Ben. My family barely made it through that time. We borrowed money to get by from my wife's parents. I never want to pull a guy out of service to hurt him financially, but it is my job now to look for unsafe conditions and violations of the rules. When I first became a road foreman in Evansville, Rocko threw a switch and didn't line it back to its original position. The oncoming train stopped short of a head-on collision with the train the Indian was on. I didn't pull Rocko out of service. I knew that one more incident at that time would have had Rocko fired in all capacities. He was on drugs, everyone knew it, and he had made other mistakes, dangerous ones. A yardmaster had Rocko sent to rehabilitation for another incident when he failed a drug test shortly after the switch failure. After eight months on the street for the violation he bumped here for a new start. I don't think the Indian ever forgave Rocko for the incident or me for not pulling him out of service. The Indian was also hopping mad that Rocko got all the good runs and didn't like working with the man. Even though the engineers' board was not affected by the dispatching irregularities the engineers were tired of the legitimate complaints of other conductors. I don't know if I made the right decision then or not concerning Rocko's rule infraction. Rocko was sent to get help several days after the incident so I thought it proved to be the right decision on my part. Also, I didn't pull the Indian out of service for revenge for his accusations of what he thought were my bad decisions. The Indian was in violation, a clear restricted speed violation in the yard."

"Did you explain all of this to John?"

"No, I just answered his questions. As I answered them I got madder and madder and walked out of his office."

"I think you better explain the situation to John just as you have to me. It will work out, Ed, you'll see."

"Thanks, Ben. We'll talk later."

"Yep," I said and hit the end call button.

I sat and thought about our conversation. It explained Ed's behavior and I felt some relief in the feeling that Ed was not involved in the murder of Rocko. A moment later my phone rang and I jumped. It was the railroad and I was to be on the W222 with my favorite conductor Lurch, again, in two hours.

Just then Deb returned to the TV room. "Was that your work call?" she asked.

"Yep, working with Lurch but we have an hour of TV. What do you want to watch?"

She looked at her watch and said *Jeopardy*.

It wasn't my favorite but I conceded since I would soon be leaving for the railyard.

Deb added, "Trish said the first week in June would be great for a visit."

"Good! I'm looking forward to the visit and getting some time off."

Deb answered an entire category correctly while I answered only one question correctly and that answer was "What is the son's name on the *Simpsons*." Oh well, I can't be good at everything I thought as Deb changed the TV channel to *Magnum PI*.

I watched half of *Magnum* and got up to pack for tonight's run. After Deb cleaned up the kitchen she packed a bag of meatloaf sandwiches for me. I grabbed the lunch and gave her a kiss on the cheek. "See you in a couple of days."

She kissed me back and off I went.

I reached the railyard and entered the office. I didn't see Lurch's truck so I apparently beat him here. That was unusual because Lurch was a timely guy with the exception of a few times he overslept at the hotel end. I saw the Indian in the locker room and greeted him. He said he wouldn't get pulled out of service because they couldn't get the speed tapes back in time for his investigation. I told him I was glad to hear it. He went on to add that Ed Lawson was a no-good son of a gun, not using that language. I asked him if he were speeding. He responded with, "You know me, Ben. Would I have been speeding through this yard?" He laughed and went out the door.

I grabbed my jacket, shut the locker and followed, feeling a bit uneasy about the Indian now.

As I was pouring a cup of coffee, Lurch came flying in. He said, "Be ready in a minute, Ben."

"It's okay. I'll grab the paperwork," I replied. I went to the computer and got our paperwork, checked that everything was there and walked out the door toward the locomotive. I heard the long strides of Lurch quickly catching up to me. He grabbed my grip tossed it up then tossed his own up. I thanked him and handed over the paperwork. "Looks good for tonight," I said as I heaved myself up that big first step.

Lurch began walking the train and I began my preparations to leave. About ten minutes later we were both in the locomotive. The dispatcher gave permission to move and we began our trip toward Saint Louis. We passed over the bridges where the two deaths had occurred and were picking up speed obeying the signals for our exit of the area. I began telling Lurch what I had learned concerning the runs that were being improperly dispatched in Evansville and what I thought was going on between Richard Hines and Rocko. I wanted to see if Lurch thought it was a correct assumption. He agreed.

We rode in silence for a while. I knew he was thinking about the case and I thought I would allow him time to process the information. He broke the silence by asking me what I knew, if anything additional, about Ed Lawson.

I relayed the conversation I had with Ed just before I left home. Lurch just shook his big head slowly. Silence followed, broken only by Lurch's calling of signals. I didn't want to break his train of thought so I just peered out into the darkness, letting the man beside me think.

He finally broke his silence saying, "The Indian really didn't like Rocko. I was on a trip with him when Rocko first arrived on our pool. He couldn't say enough negative comments about Rocko. That surprised me. The Indian usually wasn't that negative concerning other trainmen. Maybe the negativity was because of the switch incident in Evansville. The Indian has the Evansville connection and certainly hated Rocko. The discussion he had with Ed was one of expressed hate for Rocko, rather than hate for Ed. Do you think the Indian could be the murderer, Ben?"

"I don't want to think so. We need to find out where the Indian was the night of the murder. I would also like to find out what was being delivered or picked up, most likely illegally, at the industry on those Evansville runs that were being dispatched to Rocko."

We continued over the tracks at a rate of sixty miles per hour. Lurch continued calling the signals. We spoke little. I was thinking about Rocko and Richard Hines. We were not dispatched into a siding on this run so my meatloaf sandwiches stayed in my grip. We even got a restricted signal into the yard. We made it to the Saint Louis yard in six hours and thirty minutes, Great run! Off duty at 0400 EST. It was really 0300 in Saint Louis. Sometimes when waking in Saint Louis we can be fooled by looking at the clocks there. More than one trainman has been an hour late for duty.

We had to wait on our van to the hotel. Lurch and I talked with an outbound crew who was waiting on their paperwork. They were from a foreign railroad and were going to take our train on west. The engineer named Tom Piper, or Pipes for short, was pleasant and talkative. He spoke of some of the changes that were coming, like automated train control and possibility of no conductors on board most trains.

"We've been warned of the same changes coming our way," I said to Pipes as Lurch looked quite pensive. The "no conductors" part must have had him worried.

Pipes's conductor walked into the crew room and seemed to not want to speak tonight. Pipes said in a hushed tone that no conductor would be better than the one he had for tonight's run. Both Lurch and I looked at Tom with confused looks on our faces. He continued in a whisper that his conductor was stoned as usual. Just then the computer started spitting out their paperwork and I told Pipes to have a safe trip.

After I heard the yard office door close I told Lurch that even though the railroads had random drug testing and some people were still trying to beat the system, sooner or later they would get caught. The yardmaster called and said our van had just pulled into the yard. We both grabbed our grips and went to meet the van.

"Hey, Betty," I greeted our driver. She was smoking outside the van as usual. She put out her butt on a nearby rock on the edge of the parking lot.

"Hi, Ben, how's it going for you and the big guy here?" she responded.

"Fine. We had a great run and are ready for sleep. You seem chipper tonight."

"That cinder dick out of Indianapolis told me that I was no longer a suspect in Rocko's murder and to just go on and do my usual good job. He isn't such a bad guy."

"John is a pretty good one. And I'm glad to see you're back to your old self again."

Betty drove quite efficiently to our home away from home, the hotel. The automatic door opened and we picked up our cookies and room keys and headed to our rooms. Mine was on the first floor this time. Lurch went up the elevator. I unpacked my meatloaf sandwiches and had my lunch then laid down for some shuteye. As I hit the hay the word "drugs" came to mind.

CHAPTER 19

SAINT LOUIS,
APRIL 1, 1230 EST

The phone signaled me awake. I answered, mumbling out my name. It was Lurch. He apologized for waking me then asked if I would come downstairs and meet him for lunch, he had some ideas about the case to discuss with me. I agreed and began my morning ministrations.

About thirty minutes had passed and I was ready to walk down the hall and meet Lurch for lunch, and it was really "lunch" time. Lurch and I decided to get in the old jalopy and drive to the Big Apple restaurant. Once we reached the restaurant we ordered Philadelphia cheese steak sandwiches and fries. Lurch said we needed to focus our investigative minds on the Indian. That he had talked with two of his friends earlier this morning and found out that the Indian was off duty the early morning of the murder. He had opportunity.

"The Indian hated Rocko," Lurch said, "perhaps because of the near train collision caused by Rocko's error, or perhaps other reasons." Lurch was certain that the Indian had motive and opportunity. "I know from some of our talks on past trains runs that he knew how to use a gun. The Indian went hunting whenever he could and got a kick out of target practice."

"I'd like to speak again with the Indian. Ask him why he had bumped from Evansville to the Indianapolis west board? And get a feeling about the degree of animosity between the two men," I replied as I dipped a single French fry into catchup. "Thanks for finding out if the Indian had the opportunity," I added. "I'm going to call my dispatcher friend and find out what was being shipped in the cars at the industry or picked up. He may know. I can give him the train symbols of the runs now. With any luck, we should know the details by tomorrow."

"Keep me in the loop, Ben." Lurch finished the last bite of his sandwich. "Should we order some pie?"

"Of course," I replied. We waited several minutes for our waitress to return and ordered our favorite slices of pie, the specialty of this restaurant. She returned with a slice of coconut cream for Lurch with the meringue piled five inches high and for me a slice of apple, looking like Mom used to bake. We enjoyed our desserts and returned to the hotel. I was in my room when the work call came in. We were to report for our train in two hours. It would be a supper run into the night and most probably a long night, stopping at several industries, and being pulled into sidings to allow the van trains to go by.

I had an hour before I had to get the van ride to the train. I decided to call Dave Colbert and see if he knew what was being delivered to the industry north of Evansville, near Roselake. Dave answered on the third ring. I announced my identity and told him I had some additional questions concerning his dispatcher days. I gave Dave the train call numbers, N893 and S461.

He thought for a while then said, "I think it was bone dust that was being delivered, Ben. I'm not completely sure but I think they were just bringing back two empty cars on the S461. The industry uses bone dust as a filter to purify a liquid product. "

"Thanks, Dave. I'm not sure what to make of all the random details I've collected but I sure appreciate your help."

"Any time old man, any time. Have a safe trip back home." Dave chuckled as he hung up.

I thought that he and I would have to get together soon and just talk. He really was a nice guy. I hung up and texted Deb to warn her of my impending arrival. I had a half hour to watch a rerun. I chose *Gunsmoke* which was halfway through. Matt Dillon was hot on the trail. I grabbed my grip and headed for the automatic doors. There to greet me in his van was Chuck, our limo driver.

I beat Lurch to the van so I took the front seat. Chuck looked good and sounded good. He said his wife was doing well, no more cancer. I was glad to hear the news. We were talking when Lurch startled us by throwing his grip in and bending his lanky frame into the back seat. He can be quite alarming at times. "You scared us to death, Lurch," I said.

"It's just me, Ben. Hi, Chuck," he said hurt by our frightened response, "Who were you guys expecting, anyway?" he asked.

"You, I guess," I said and asked Chuck if he would stop at the sandwich shop. Chuck complied and I bought him a sandwich along with mine since he was my favorite driver. Lurch bought himself a turkey club and off we went to the railyard. When we arrived, our paperwork was ready. Lurch grabbed it and we walked to our big old slop train. It was long and heavy. It was also slow due to lack of power so any van train out there tonight would have the right of way and we would be sitting alongside as it passed. Long night!

We pulled out of the yard as the sun was setting behind us. It seemed as I increased my speed the sun neared the horizon to our rear and darkness began to fill the eastern sky like blackberry jelly being poured into a jar. As we were making our way through Illinois I told Lurch what Dave Colbert had to say concerning the cars set out in Roselake. He shook his head and sat in his seat with gears turning in that great big head of his. My gears were turning too.

We approached our first industry and I slowed the big slop train as we pulled in. Lurch had to do some work now and set out eight cars. I waited to hear from him on the radio as he walked the train. We sat at this industry several more hours and ate our sub sandwiches. After given permission to leave I finally got our speed up to forty miles per hour. I could go fifty but the power wasn't sufficient for the weight of the train.

We were moving at this rate when we rounded a curve and spotted a tanker truck on the tracks. It took only a moment to realize it wasn't moving off the tracks at a crossing. With only seconds to impact I pulled the emergency brake and yelled "hit the floor!"

There was no way this train would stop before the impending crash. This was every trainmen's nightmare, hitting a fuel tanker and blowing up both truck and locomotive. I had but a second to think this was our last train run in this life.

I prepared for the coming crash as best I could as the jar of the crash forced me forward on the locomotive floor, my body was thrust into the metal of the engine just as the windshield was blown out.. The next instant I felt slimy goo covering my body and wondered what part of leaving this world was slimy goo.

I began to realize I was still alive as I heard Lurch speaking words I had never heard come out of him. I looked over and there before me was a six-foot, seven-inch slime-covered monster.

We were alive and covered in corn syrup! From head to foot we were covered in a sticky, clear liquid. Our entire smashed up locomotive was covered in a translucent, fly-catching syrup. It had been forced through every crevice in the engine, it covered the inside of the cab. It covered the catwalk and cow catcher. The entire steel locomotive was now badly misshapen.

As we surveyed the damage and each other we began to laugh, just plain belly laugh. I laughed until tears poured forth. I hadn't even realized that I was pretty bruised and cut from being forced against the steel walls of the locomotive. We survived our biggest fear, running into a tanker truck, and we were all the sweeter for it.

My radio still worked, wonder of wonders, and I called for assistance. Lurch had tried to get down off the engine, but the floor was too slippery to move safely. We were stuck there like two lollipops, one chubby, one tall, standing upright on this misshapen candy-coated steel mess.

Eventually help arrived. Firemen, policemen, and paramedics all seemed to go about their work with smirks on their faces as they attempted to provide safe egress for Lurch and I to disembark the locomotive. It seemed the driver of the tanker ran from the scene and had been arrested for his part in what came to be later known as the Great Misadventure of the Willie Wonka Express. Lurch and I were really not too badly damaged. But it took a day and a half for our locomotive to be pulled away from the train because of its slippery coating.

We were checked out at the local hospital, allowed to shower, released, and van-driven home. The guys cheered for us as we entered the Indianapolis yard office, even management cheered. I was anxious to just get home to my wife and call this trip over.

When I got home it was almost 12:00. Deb was not home. So, I changed into shorts and a T-shirt and laid down for shuteye. Every ounce of energy had been drained from my body after the adrenaline rush during our misadventure. My body was bruised and sore, my left leg had a particularly large and deep purple bruise on the outer calf muscle, so it didn't take but half a second for me to be under the influence of blessed sleep.

I was jerked awake, suddenly, by a bad dream that my train had run headlong into another. My heart was pounding rapidly, I was gasping for air, and head pounding. I got up and went in to splash some water on my face and tried to calm down. After a few minutes, I felt my blood pressure and heart rate returning to normal. I decided to check the time and found that it was 1900. I walked out in the kitchen. No arresting aromas, no Deb. She did, however, leave a note on the table.

Ben,
Glad to see you are at home. There is a meal of chicken, mashed potatoes and peas in the microwave. Just heat for two minutes. I am at church taking meeting minutes. Should be home at 9:00 or 9:30.
Love,
Deb

I heated my dinner and took it into the TV room. I turned on the television and found an English murder mystery on PBS. I knew if Deb returned she would like this one as well. I was nearly finished with my meal when I heard the garage door open. I was glad to hear that welcoming sound. Deb came into the TV room and kissed my nearly bald head.

"We finished our meeting a bit early tonight. Some of the ministry leaders were not able to make it, so reports were short," she said as she sat on her chair. "How was your trip?" she asked.

"I thought you would never ask. I'm surprised you didn't notice the bruise on my lower leg. Boy! Do I have a story to tell you," I responded and then proceeded to recount the Misadventure of the Willie Wonka Express.

She glanced down at my leg but was speechless, then said she was so glad I was alive. Then she got tears in her eyes. She kissed me for real and I felt her tears. She was silent and I was silent. It was good to see that she cared. We really did need to thank God for another day of life in this world. We did just that and turned off the TV and the lights and went to bed.

CHAPTER 20

INDIANAPOLIS, APRIL 2, 0730 EST

awoke to the smell of bacon cooking. Nothing like the aroma of bacon to get me vertical. It took but a second to get to the kitchen. There being plated before me were three slices of bacon, two eggs over easy, two slices of wheat toast and a big scoop of fried potatoes. The kitchen smelled heavenly. Deb finished the whole thing off by pouring me a big cup of coffee, with, of all things, half and half. I knew this was a special day. "What's with the gourmet breakfast?" I asked.

"Celebrating life, Ben. Celebrating life."

I waited for Deb to sit and we said grace and continued celebrating. She said she would be going into work today. I said I was three times out and wasn't sure whether I would be home when she returned or be off to work. She gave me a good smooch and she left. I was on clean-up duty. It took me about fifteen minutes to put the kitchen back in order. Then I took my second cup of coffee into the TV room.

I sat and thought about the murder case. It seemed that Lurch thought the Indian was our key suspect and I was reluctant to think he was capable of murder. I got my notes out and began to read them over when the phone began to ring. Caller ID indicated it was John from the railroad police department.

"Hi, John. How is everything going?" I asked.

"Not bad, Ben. I heard through the grapevine you have been diving into corn syrup. Are you all right?"

"Just a little bruised and battered, now slime free, and glad to be alive."

"Good to hear, Ben. I sure don't want anything to happen to my best investigator. I heard that they got the driver of the tanker truck. He had failed a sobriety test and had an arrest record for transporting drugs. I guess he saw how close your train was and panicked. Good thing it was syrup and not any number of combustibles."

"I'll tell you the complete story from the cab's eye view next time I'm in, John. Now to change the subject, can you tell me anything more about the relationship between the Indian and Rocko?" I asked.

"I've interviewed the Indian, several times now. He made it clear that he didn't care for Rocko, but said that he was no killer. I may be calling him in again for questioning. What do you think?"

"Lurch and I were talking and determined that the Indian did have means, motive and opportunity. I would like to talk with the Indian and get a feeling for how intense the dislike between the two men was. But you know, John, there could be one or two killers out there. It doesn't necessarily follow that one man killed Rocko and pushed Hines from the Danville bridge or maybe Hines' death was accidental. There could be two different men involved."

"I've been thinking along those lines as well."

"Were you aware that it was bone dust being left at the industry in Roselake and empty cars being returned to Evansville? I just checked this out with a retired dispatcher friend of mine. I'm not sure what it means but it may have some significance."

"Thanks for the additional facts, Ben. And I'm glad you're still with us."

"I'm glad too. Talk to you later. I may be in soon. I'm three times out."

"Okay, Ben. Talk Later."

I hung up and decided to reread my notes. I thought I must be missing something. After rereading the notes, I decided to get dressed. I was looking for a finger nail clipper and couldn't find mine but remembered I had one with my fishing gear. I opened the tackle box and found the clippers near a new lure I had bought last spring. It was still in the box. I often hid my new lures with my old but I should have taken it out of the box to really keep it hidden. I clipped the offending nail and took the lure out of its new box so it would be soundly camouflaged with the old ones. My wife thought lures were a waste of money and my addiction.

After I finished dressing I went back to my notes. I thought about bone dust being delivered to the industry and wondered what could be hidden in it. What could be camouflaged? The white powder could, indeed, hide cocaine among many other substances. Like hides like. White powder can hide white powder. In addition, I took note that the word "drugs" had been recurring in this investigation.

I decided to talk to Ed and ask him what drug was causing Rocko his problems. Or maybe ask the Indian if he knew which drug was causing Rocko his problems. Asking the Indian would allow me to get a feeling for his animosity toward Rocko, maybe kill two birds with one stone. So, I decided I would give the Indian a call. I dialed the stand number. The computerized system would give me information concerning the Indian's last call. I would know if he was on duty or where he was currently, in Saint Louis or Indianapolis. After listening carefully to all the information, I knew the Indian was in Saint Louis and completed his last run last night. He should be rested so I gave him a call.

He picked up on the second ring. "Hey, Big Ben. Thanks for shutting down the whole railroad for a day. I'm stuck here and will be going to the boat to give away some money. Heard you and the big guy were sticky messes."

"We were. I'm glad to oblige you in handling your free time."

"Seriously, were you hurt?"

"No just bruised and shaken. Really, I'm just glad to be alive, Indian. I thought I was a goner when I saw that tanker at the crossing. There was no time to stop the slop train I had."

"I know what you mean. I've had bad dreams about being unable to stop a train myself. I'm glad you are all right. Hey, what are you calling for, anyway?"

"I've been thinking about Rocko's death. Do you know what drug or drugs he was having problems with before he was sent to rehab?"

"Cocaine was his drug of choice. He nearly got me killed once. He shouldn't have been allowed to work out there. He left a switch in the yard misaligned and I was nearly blasted into by another locomotive. The man was a menace and everyone knew it. Ed Lawson should have made sure the man never worked again in our industry. I can't say that I'm distraught over the man's demise, but I'm no killer. Is that what you wanted to hear?"

"To be honest, that is what I wanted to hear. But, as an aside, I think your beef with Ed is a little skewed. He has to follow company rules."

"He didn't, Ben. Rocko should have been pulled off the property at once. He was higher than a kite and could have killed both myself and the conductor. Ed failed to follow the rules. Then he tries to pull me out of service for a speed violation. What kind of consistency is that?"

"You may have a point. Maybe Rocko should have been pulled out of service that day in Evansville but he was pulled out several days later."

"No thanks to Ed Lawson."

"Ed Lawson has been one of the few in management reluctant to pull guys out of service. I would hate to be here if there were more eager managers to see us on the streets. Just think about it. Just think about a few of the past road foreman."

"I'll think about it, but I don't think I will change my mind about the guy."

"Okay, Indian. You have a good day and I'll talk to you later."

"Yep, talk later, Oh, I heard your new nickname is now Willie Wonka."

"Roger that."

I hung up on the Indian hoping I had planted a seed for a more harmonious relationship between the Indian and Ed.

Then I sat and thought about the case. It was hard for me to believe that the man I just spoke with was a killer. I tried to piece what may have happened that night two men were found dead near two different bridges. After some time, I thought that a most probable conclusion was that Richard Hines hired Rocko to set certain cars out at Roselake for a drug transfer for either delivery or pick up or both. It would be necessary for a conductor to be on the take rather than an engineer since the conductor is responsible for setting out the cars. That would explain why only Rocko was getting those runs and the engineer's board was not being dispatched incorrectly. Rocko was either taking pay from Hines in the form of cash or drugs. It could also explain the inscription on the expensive watch, "Thanks for the High Times." It was probably a gift from Hines. I could not match the killing of Rocko with Sudsy, Ed, or the Indian. However, Hines was in the area that night. Perhaps he killed Rocko. But why would he kill his employee?

I was getting the feeling I was on the right track so I decided to give my buddy, Lurch, a call and run this theory by him. I was glad he answered on the second ring.

"Hi, Lurch, this is Ben. Do you have a few minutes so I can run my theory by you?"

"He said, "Shoot, Ben."

I repeated my latest theory to Lurch.

He listened. Then said, "You're thinking it probably wasn't the Indian, as the murderer and Rocko's death had something to do with his involvement with drugs with Hines, correct?"

"Yes."

"But why would Hines want his employee dead?" Lurch asked.

"I'm not sure. I need some more facts. I need to know more about Hines," I said.

"Hines bid on to our board as a crew dispatcher using his seniority. Do you think Rocko was threatening him or refusing to work for him in his new-found sobriety? Could that explain Hines wanting Rocko dead?"

"Either could explain Hines being out at the bridge that night and wanting Rocko dead. But who wanted Hines dead? Hines could have shot Rocko at the haunted bridge and then drove down to the Danville bridge.

Why would he want to be there? And who would he be meeting with? It wasn't Rocko. He was already dead."

Lurch thought quietly for some minutes then said, "I think if Rocko was truly no longer on drugs and wanted a new beginning, a new start, he would have refused to work for Hines. I think Hines may have gotten nervous and shot his ex-partner. Perhaps he was going to meet with a new partner at the Danville bridge. You know, Ben, we set out two cars at the Danville industry on the W267 and often are idled on or near the Danville bridge. It is a similar set up to the industry in Roselake. This is all starting to make some sense. I think Hines was checking out the bridge, industry, and a new partner!"

"I think we're on to something. Who could the new partner be? It would have to be someone on the west board, our board, and a conductor. One of your own kind, Lurch."

"Well, we can take me off the list. I'll be thinking about this, Ben and looking for any flaws in our logic. And then get back to you. But you know, you work with the conductors and know them better than I do. I work with the engineers. So, think about them. There are fourteen on the board and you can cross me off. That leaves thirteen possibilities as drug partners with Hines."

"I'll be thinking, and will probably be back to work on a night run tonight. How many times out are you?"

"I'm five times out so you'll probably be with one of the possibilities on our list, Ben. Take care."

I told Lurch I would take care too and then hung up. I sat in the recliner thinking of our conversation.

I don't believe our logic was flawed even though there were definitely some leaps and bounds taken. I called the stand number just to hear a list of the conductors on the west bound board. There were no surprises. All men I've worked with many times. Now I was thinking that one of them was considering working with Hines, considering drug deliveries, and may also be a killer. I decided I needed some sleep before my next run and went into my pad. It didn't take but two minutes to fall into a deep sleep.

The phone blasted and I came to life. I garbled out my response. "Ben Time here."

It was an automated voice informing me to be on a train, the W879, in the usual two hours, at 1700 EST with Sudsy as my conductor. I pressed the numeral two to indicate I accepted the call and rose for my shower.

The shower got me alert and as I packed my grip I began thinking about my conversation with Lurch. I wanted to give him a call to find out if he still thought our theory valid but I dared not because he was probably sleeping. I walked out to see if Deb was home and to my good luck, she was.

She had heard the phone ring and assumed it was my work call so she packed me a lunch/supper. We sat at the kitchen table and discussed our day's events.

Deb, with a look of concern in her eyes, asked how I was feeling

I responded, "Fine, ready to take hold of the levers once again." However, secretly I wasn't so sure that was true.

She continued, "I don't know why they won't give you a day of recovery before you go out again."

"The less the company makes over this, the less likely they feel they will get sued. The company will eventually take statements and hope that my conductor and I have no lasting injuries or litigious intentions. It's probably better I get back up on the horse anyway." I then stood, pushed my chair in, and asked, "What's for lunch tonight?"

"Taco soup in the Mason jar and some French bread, and apple slices."

I thanked her for the lunch, gave her a kiss good bye and was out the door. I wanted to get to the yard a bit early and talk to John if possible.

As I turned onto the main road I thought about my lunch. I loved the taco soup and could put it on the heater in the locomotive compartment. Then at a siding have warm nourishment. It was going to be a good night tonight, I thought, as I drove toward the Indianapolis yard.

When I got to the yard office I saw John in his office still working. I rapped lightly on the open door. He looked up and greeted me. "Welcome, Captain of the Willie Wonka Express."

I responded, "Funny, John. Can we talk?" I had decided to talk out our theory with him before I got onto my locomotive. John listened without a word then said, "Be careful, Ben. I don't see any information in my reports that contradicts your theory but I don't see the evidence, yet, either. Just take care out there. And I'll keep looking into this."

I stood up and gave the man a salute as I left his office. I saw Sudsy at the computer getting the last of our paperwork. "Hey, Big Ben, or should I hail you as Willie Wonka?"

I guessed I wouldn't hear the end of this misadventure for a while.

"Hi, Sudsy, are we ready to take off?" I asked trying to ignore the greeting.

He nodded his head in the affirmative and we both turned and headed for the yard office door. Our train was rumbling in the yard, it was nearby for a change. I threw my grip up the steps and Sudsy threw his up. I lifted my own self up that daunting first step and Sudsy began walking the train. When I stood at the controls I suddenly had a flashback of the tanker stranded at the crossing. A shiver went down my spine as I began my preparations for this trip, trying with great effort to ignore the fear that was seeping into my body. I just needed to tackle this and get back up on this horse, I told myself. I completed the "three-step protection"—checking the automatic break was fully applied, the generator field breaker was down, and the independent and automatic brakes fully applied to protect the conductor as he walked the train releasing hand brakes on the first six cars—and Sudsy did his part. The train dispatcher gave us permission to leave the yard. So far so good, I told myself as my lead locomotive moved forward, pulling the long train behind. I looked at my watch and noticed we left on time, a good start.

As we crossed the haunted bridge, the sun was setting. The impending darkness started me thinking about the case once again. I looked over at Sudsy wondering if he was thinking along those lines as well. Sudsy was fiddling with his paperwork looking down rather than forward to call out signals. I asked him if he had any ideas who might have killed Rocko. He looked up at me with a fearful look in eyes and looked back down very quickly, shaking his head negatively. I was surprised at his response. I knew he was cleared of Rocko's death.

It took only about ten minutes to reach the Danville bridge. I decided to question Sudsy more concerning the bridge deaths. "Have you ever had Hines as a dispatcher? Did he ever call you out for a job?"

"Once or twice he called me out. At least I think it was him," Sudsy responded in a very low tone. I had difficulty hearing his answer.

"I heard he miscalled a lot of conductors down in Evansville. He made a lot of enemies, I guess. Did you notice any miscalls yet?"

Sudsy shook his head, no, and called the next signal. As I pulled on the throttle to get the beast up to speed, we passed another clear signal. I decided to continue questioning Sudsy since I had him trapped in our locomotive for the night. "I hadn't heard the guys complaining either but Hines had just recently been dispatching our runs."

Sudsy looked over at me and spoke in a loud and aggressive tone. "I'm not in the mood for small talk, Ben. I'll call the signals and you run the engine!"

I was surprised by this. I knew he had a temper but he hadn't used it on me in all our runs. I quieted and began once again thinking, could this be the man who killed Hines? If Hines approached Sudsy to be his new partner would Sudsy actually agree to be involved in drugs? Would he meet with Hines? Did they meet and fight? How could I get this guy to open up? More and more questions kept popping into my mind along these lines.

I was quiet for some time. I noticed we had made it to Illinois and were about to set several cars out at the first industry. We went about our respective responsibilities and soon Sudsy was back up in the locomotive. According to the dispatcher we were going to wait for the W676 to pass by before we would be given permission to resume travel. I decided to warm my soup and begin eating my dinner.

Sudsy broke the silence between us and commented on how good the soup smelled. I offered him some in his thermos cup and he ate/drank it greedily. While he was walking the train, I had decided my best bet would be to just tell him Lurch and John shared that theory. I figured just in case this man had something to do with Hines's death he would be aware that others besides me had heard the theory. Self-preservation was my motive. So, I started telling my theory, beginning with Rocko's part in past drug deals and ending in Hines's searching for another partner.

Sudsy listened to my whole theory then peered far out into the night for some five minutes. He opened his mouth and no sound came out. Then he opened his mouth again.

"Ben, your theory is for the most part correct. Hines contacted me by phone to set out cars at the Danville industry. He said on the phone it would be simple. I just had to make sure that the cars were set out on the right track when no one was around. I would not be placing drugs in the cars. Someone else would do that."

I looked up from my computer screens at a man trying to excuse very bad decisions. He began to speak more rapidly as he rationalized his thinking.

"I was just to make sure the cars were there and no one else was there to steal from them. Just do my job. I would get paid per job and get the run. It all looked good at first. I needed to make up for the money I lost when Rocko bumped my position and I went back to the extra-board for work. I had told myself that I wouldn't be handling the drugs, that I would be just doing my job for some extra pay."

Sudsy looked remorseful as he continued. "I agreed at first to the job and agreed to meet Hines at the bridge. He was there measuring the distance from the industry to what normally would be the position of the lead engine. It had to be far enough from the cars being delivered and conductor so there would be no chance that the conductor could be seen by the engineer. I went with him, we were on the Danville bridge and I suddenly got a conscience. Bad timing. I wanted nothing to do with drug delivery. I told him that much and he turned to hit me. We fought and he fell from the bridge. I don't think

I pushed him, Ben, I really don't think I pushed him." Sudsy suddenly put his head in his hands and sobbed out, "I don't know what to do."

I was surprised by the revelation and yet not. I sat in the dark and asked him, "Did Hines mention anything about Rocko that made you think he killed the man?"

Sudsy thought and stared out into the night then finally said, "Hines said that Rocko used his extra cash for drugs and said that maybe I could use mine more wisely. Then he said, 'Oh well, no more high times for Rocko, no more time for Rocko.' At that moment, I thought Hines meant that Rocko was just quitting drugs or the drug delivery job, not that Rocko had been shot to death. However, that was probably the statement that got my conscience working. I didn't like Rocko nor did I want to be like him. What should I do, Ben?"

I was quiet for a minute then said, "You better tell this to John. I don't think it would be a murder charge since you fought with Hines in self-defense and he fell and you hadn't delivered any cars for drug transfer. You'll probably need a lawyer, though. I'll help where I can, Sudsy."

We were given permission to continue our run. It was silent for the most part. When we arrived at 0500 EST at the Saint Louis yard, my conductor asked if I would call John for him. Sudsy would tell him the truth of his early morning several weeks back.

I agreed to make the call when we got into our hotel rooms.

CHAPTER 21

SAINT LOUIS,
APRIL 3, 0500 EST

I didn't have to yard the train and pulled up on track number two. We then tied the train down. I gathered up my things and placed them in my grip. Sudsy did the same. We dismounted and walked slowly toward the office. It didn't take long to put our time slips into the computer and go to the van.

Betty was waiting, taking her last long drag of nicotine before she would drive us to the hotel. I greeted her and she exhaled loudly, producing a ring of smoke. She sure had perfected her habit through some sixty years of smoking. She climbed in the van and off we went to the hotel. It was a very quick trip this time of day, no traffic clogging up our way. It occurred to me that Sudsy may have wished it to be a much longer trip to the hotel. Once we arrived and got our room keys I asked Sudsy to meet me in my room at 0700. It would be 8:00 AM in

Indianapolis and I knew John would be on duty. He was always punctual. I threw my grip on the queen bed. It didn't even bounce. I guessed that this room had a very firm mattress. I washed up so I could remain awake for the next couple of hours. The cool water did the trick. I turned on the TV to hear the morning news. It was going to be a perfect spring morning here in Saint Louis. After two commercials advertising lawyers who would handle medical malpractice suits I turned off the set. I thought that just knowing it would be a beautiful spring day was enough. I heard a rap on the door and opened it to see Sudsy looking at me with anxious eyes. I didn't say a word. He just walked in and sat on the overstuffed chair. I took the office chair in front of the desk. I pushed in the pass code on my phone and searched the contacts for John. I looked at Sudsy and asked him if he was ready and he nodded in the affirmative. I dialed John and he answered on the third ring. I greeted the man and told him I had Susy with me and he had some information about Hines's death he needed to pass on and that John would most likely want to record. John asked if I could wait a minute while he hooked up his recorder. We waited. It seemed like a very long time but I was sure it was only a few minutes. I put Sudsy on the phone and he began his recounting of that early morning several weeks ago.

He recounted the incident in a monotone voice, showing no emotion, as I sat very still watching a man's life about to change, perhaps for a very long time.

Sudsy said, "That's all," and then hung up. He rose slowly from the overstuffed chair and shut my door very quietly behind him as he left.

Rocko's life ended tragically just as he was gaining freedom from an addiction. Sudsy may get out of this okay, but his momentary greed may still cost him dearly. I was glad that Ed and the Indian were not involved. Hines, the killer and the drug runner, lost his life. I wondered how many lives his drugs destroyed and who will take his place transferring the evil that steals, kills, and destroys so many in our country.

Just as I was thinking, my phone rang. It was Deb.

"Hey, Ben, I hope I'm not disturbing your rest but I wanted to ask if you would be home tomorrow morning?"

"I'm not sure yet. I just got in. I'll have to check my stand number. Why?"

She answered, "It's Easter Sunday and I wondered if we would be attending church together?"

"Wow. Easter already. After I get some sleep, I'll check my stand number and text you on my estimated time of arrival, okay? Oh, and I think Lurch and I solved the case of the twin bridges and bodies. I'll fill you in when I get home."

"Can't wait. I will definitely sleep better. Are you sure you can't fill me in now?"

"I don't have time to do the explanation justice. Besides, now I can be assured you will be looking forward to my return."

"I always look forward to your return. Love you, Ben. Hope to see you tomorrow early!"

I had a lot to be thankful for. Deb had a way of bringing me back to better things, to home, family and to God. I wasn't sure if I would make it home in time for Resurrection Day service but I knew that I was thankful that I was a recipient of the Resurrection Day blessing.

ABOUT THE AUTHOR

    Tammi Huggins is an Indiana author, residing in Avon, Indiana for the majority of the year and in the North Tampa area for the winter months, although born and raised in Northwest Pennsylvania. She received her PhD in Leadership Administration in Higher Education from Indiana State University and is the author of "Murder and Misconception," the first in the Ben Time Mystery series. In addition, she has published over fifty Christian articles for various denominations and is a Christian speaker. Tammi is married to a retired locomotive engineer and has two adult daughters.

CPSIA information can be obtained
at www.ICGtesting.com
Printed in the USA
BVHW031411131119
563707BV00003B/363/P